THREE FRIENDS
AND THE
MAGIC TREE WAND

THREE FRIENDS
AND THE
MAGIC TREE WAND

By Marty A. Bullis

ILLUSTRATED BY TERRY STEWART

The characters and events in this book are fictional, any
resemblance to actual persons or events is coincidental.

Printed in the United States of America
2008—First Edition

10 9 8 7 6 5 4 3 2

ISBN: 1-4392-1141-8 (paper)

For Madelen and Ryker
who magically help me discover each day

CONTENTS

THE FINDING OF IT

MATTY WAS SLOWLY WAKING UP as Amos nuzzled his cold nose into her face. Ryker still lay asleep at her feet, his red hair blowing in the cool breeze. The clouds were passing quickly over their resting place on Mole Hill, while the sun was starting to set on this early spring day.

They knew they weren't supposed to be here. The Mennonite man who owned the hill didn't like people wandering around on it because his cows grazed in this area. But it was a quiet place for the three friends, and they would often sneak away to look for volcanic rocks at the top. Today they had left the house after lunch. It was Saturday and they had spent the afternoon exploring the hill, and then had lain down for a nap. Mole Hill was the only volcano in this part of the country. It was a small hill now, because erosion had worn it down over millions of years. A geologist once told them the volcano was extinct, but they often wondered what would happen if it erupted again.

Amos saw that Matty was now awake. He didn't sleep soundly when they were outdoors. It was his job to protect everyone—to be on the lookout for danger—and he knew it. So, he had been resting his nose on Matty's chest as she dozed, scanning the hillside for any movement.

Matty loved Amos. She had never known a time without her dog. He was nine years old—not so very fast anymore, but he could be fierce if he needed to be. Once when Matty and Ryker were hiking in the National Forest with their parents, they came around a bend and startled a bear eating berries. As always, Amos was at the front of the family pack. He stopped to let everyone know there was trouble. Perking up his ears, he began to growl deep in his throat—standing his ground to let the bear know not to come near. The bear didn't come near, but it didn't move away either, so Amos started barking ferociously and baring his teeth. The old bear finally got the idea that Amos meant business. Not wanting to fight an angry dog, the bear moved off the trail and down the hill. Amos followed it a short distance to make sure everything would be safe for his Matty and the rest of the family.

That's how Matty always felt with Amos—safe. She hugged him around the neck and kissed the top of his wet nose. "I love you Amos," she said, then stretched her arms, yawned wide, and looked about the hill. "I guess we'd better wake Ryker and look for some more rocks before it gets dark." The sun was getting lower in the sky, but they still had a few minutes before they would have to head back home. Matty stood up. Amos walked over to rouse Ryker.

Matty liked to scare her brother. She wasn't trying to be mean when she did it, but often an urge would overcome her and she'd try to scare the devil out of him.

"RYKER, WAKE UP!" Matty yelled. "I think the mountain is erupting!"

Now, normally this wouldn't have been a big deal. Ryker was used to this type of waking from his sister. However at this particular instant, Ryker was dreaming deeply about a roller blade hockey game. And this was no ordinary moment in his dream game. He was on the verge of scoring a goal *and* he saw that when he made the dream shot, he was going to be plowed down by a huge dream defender. Just as he got the shot off and made contact with the dream player, Matty yelled. At the same instant, Amos, who was a ready participant in Matty's pranks, pounced on Ryker. The sudden shock of an 85-pound dog landing on him, a dream defender smashing into him, and his sister's high-pitched alarm were enough to send him flying. His body, as if jolted by an electric wire, seemed to jump straight off the ground.

Matty loved every moment of this. Ryker grabbed wildly for anything he could and clenched Amos in a merciless bear-hug. Both went rolling down the hill. They were a large convulsing ball of screams and howls. The sheer energy of the whole event made it one of the best scares ever. "It was," as Matty would tell her mom later, "to die for."

When the mass of skin and fur stopped rolling, Ryker jumped to his feet in a daze. It took him a few moments to figure out where he was and what had happened. "Matty, what the heck are you trying to do . . . kill me?" he asked angrily. Matty tried not to smile, but the laughter rolled out.

"I got you *soooooo* good this time Ryker Daniel," she said. Ryker wanted to tackle her, but he knew Matty could hold her own with him. Matty was ten-and-a-half years old, and Ryker was just nine. Pretty soon he would be bigger than she was, but right now he didn't want to wrestle her if he might get stomped. Ryker liked to win.

Amos, meanwhile, was picking thistle seeds off his front legs with his teeth. When thistles would get stuck in his long fur their dad would have to cut them out with scissors. Their dad didn't seem to mind, though. He was glad the kids were out exploring with Amos instead of sitting in front of the TV or surfing the Internet.

"Come on, Ryker. I'll race you to the top of the hill," Matty said. Ryker took off instantly. He knew he could beat Matty if they started together—he was faster than she was—but he was starting down the hill a ways. She had an advantage over him. It was no surprise to him that Matty didn't wait for him to get up to her. Matty liked to win too. As soon as they started, Amos decided he needed to stop his thistle picking and get to the front of the pack. Amos passed Ryker, bumping him as he went by. It didn't take him long to get ahead of Matty and back at the head of the expedition. Amos knew they were heading to the stand of oaks at the top of the hill—their favorite place on the extinct volcano.

Amos reached the top far ahead of Matty and Ryker and started looking around for any sign of trouble. Ryker was gaining on Matty when they approached the oaks. He sure wanted to pounce on her as he got close, but paybacks come in many forms. He knew winning the race after starting so far down the hill would really get to Matty. So he poured on the speed and blew past her.

As he came to the center of the oak stand, he leapt onto the rock formation that marked the top of the hill. He turned in Matty's direction and shouted, "The uncontested winner of the Mole Hill Sky Running Competition once again is . . . drum roll please! Prrrrrrrrrrd . . . RYKER DANIEL ALDER." Matty was doing her best not to notice this show. She knew she deserved *some* retaliation, but her motto was, "Never acknowledge defeat!"

She walked over to Amos, who had seated himself next to a large white oak, and said, "Give me a high-five, Buddy." Amos threw his front paw up into her hand. "Yeah! We made it, Amos. What should we do now?"

"What should we do *now?*" Ryker said sarcastically. "You two should hail the Skyrunner."

"Oh give it a rest, Ryker, or I'll come up on that rock and thrash you," said Matty in an annoyed tone. "Let's look for some rocks, Amos," she said and turned away.

Ryker didn't push his victory any further. He knew he'd gotten her back for scaring him. So, he joined them to look for rocks. After a few minutes of searching, Ryker noticed that Amos had moved to the other side of his Sky-runner throne and was pretty interested in something. "What do you have there, Buddy?" he asked. Amos was digging next to an outcropping of rocks in some soft peaty soil. As Ryker came around the rocks, he saw that Amos had uncovered a fairly large fissure that led down into the ground. The soil had been covering the hole, so they had never seen it in their wanderings around the hill.

"What are you two doing over there?" asked Matty.

"Come over here, Matty, you've got to see this hole." Matty came cautiously. She was never sure when Ryker was finished with his paybacks. He had a habit of faking truces. She saw Amos digging at the small fissure in the ground that seemed to go down a foot or more. Then Amos lengthened the hole to expose more of it.

"What has Amos got there?" she asked.

"I don't know. But his hair is bristling, so I'm betting it's something he's not sure about."

"Maybe it's a giant mole hole on Mole Hill," Matty joked.

"Amos would love to getta hold of the mole that could make a hole *that* big," Ryker said. "I bet you it's part of the old volcano pipe. A volcano *has* to have a vent pipe some-where."

Amos continued to dig as if there were a bone in the hole. Matty and Ryker let him work at the soft soil for a few minutes. Dirt flew everywhere.

"So, who is going to give Amos a bath when we get home?" Ryker asked.

"He's your dog. Remember how you two were playing *cuddles* a few minutes ago?" Matty said in a drippy tone. Matty wasn't one for giving up so easily on paybacks herself.

Ryker said, "You're gonna get it if you don't watch it, Sis. . . . Hey, what's he got there?"

Amos had stopped digging and was pulling something up from deep in the fissure. It was long and he had to back away from the hole to get it out. Once it was out of the hole, Amos quickly ran a few feet away to enjoy his find. "What is it Matty? A bone?"

"I don't know, but we'd better see what it is. We don't want him eating anything gross!"

Ryker walked over to Amos and scratched the fuzzy spot behind his ear. He leaned down and pulled the long object out of Amos' mouth and out from under his body. (Amos had the habit of lying on big bones as he chewed them. This made it harder for someone to take the bone away from him.)

"Look at this Matty, it's a weird stick," said Ryker.

"It's really shaped strangely, and look at those colors," said Matty.

Matty took the stick from Ryker's hand and ran her fingers over it. It was about 30-inches long and polished smooth like a piece of driftwood. It was as thick as two of Matty's fingers put together, and it curved back and forth down its length.

"It reminds me of Miss Anne's little bush. What does she call that thing, Ryker?"

"It's not a bush. It's a Harry Lauder tree. Remember he was the Scottish guy with a crooked cane," Ryker told her.

"Well, whatever. The tree looks like a bush, and this stick looks like the tree."

She turned the stick around in her hands like a drill and enjoyed the feel of the corkscrewing action. The bark was all gone and two colors of wood intermingled: one red and another light cream. "This looks like a pine tree mixed up with one of those manzanita trees we saw in California," said Matty.

Amos was near Matty. He wanted his stick back. He had been watching it closely ever since Ryker had wrestled it from him. He grabbed one end of the stick in his mouth and began a tug-of-war with Matty. "No, Amos!" she said. "Stop it!" Amos dropped the stick and gave a bark. "What's up with you?" she asked.

Ryker, meanwhile, had resumed his search for rocks and was looking around the fissure. "Matty, we better get going soon. Mom told us not to be late. We're going over to Miss Sue's and Miss Anne's for dinner, and the sun's dropping."

Matty said, "All right. We can head back. It will take us a while to get home. Let's go down the far side of the hill through the little path then we can cut over to Silver Lake and on into town."

"Okay, but I'm leading the way. Are you keeping that stick Amos found?" he asked.

"Yeh. I don't know what I'll do with it. It's not long enough for a walking stick. But it feels nice in my hand," she said. "Anyhow, we'd better get going."

They walked at a good pace down one of the cow paths on the hill. Amos was blazing the trail followed by Ryker and then Matty. Matty was waving the stick behind her like a whip antenna, whacking the ground with it every so often. Something behind them darted off into the undergrowth. In an instant, Amos turned off the trail and headed back up the hill after it. "Amos," Ryker called loudly. "Come on, Buddy. We don't have time to chase squirrels now. AAAAAMOOOOSSS, COME ONNNN." He and Matty kept walking down the path. They couldn't hear Amos, but knew he would catch up.

It was getting darker as they walked. The shadows were lengthening. The sun was already out of view on this side of the hill as they walked. They heard Amos running full speed to catch up and get in the lead. Then they heard a THUMP. It sounded like Amos had taken a header onto the ground.

"Amos! Come on, friend," yelled Matty.

Amos had been running full speed down the path. He knew every turn, every rock and bush. Cows roamed up and down this path, and Amos would mark prominent obstacles. This let the cows know he had been around and it also gave him a sure roadmap of his travels. But something was not right, for as he was racing down the hill in the shadows he ran smack into a young sapling in the middle of the path. The sapling stopped him cold, knocking the wind out of him. He got up and sniffed the small tree. He had never marked this one. He circled it and stared as if thinking: *How had I missed this before? It's in the middle of the path.*

He was falling behind and didn't have time to waste. He quickly sniffed the sapling again, lifted his leg, and marked it. In a flash he was off, then back at the lead of the pack, looking for danger.

DINNER WITH THE LADIES

AS THEY PASSED SILVER LAKE near the edge of town, Matty and Ryker saw their dad, who was finishing up his evening run. He was wearing his red strobe flasher that identified him instantly. He was the only runner around who wore a strobe light, and he took a lot of grief from the neighbors about it.

Amos was on him in a second, nearly knocking him down from behind. Amos usually accompanied Mr. Alder on runs, but he had missed this one because he was out with the kids.

"Hey Buddy, where have you been?" said their dad, and turning around he saw the kids running quickly up to him on the shoulder of the road. As they got closer, their dad slowed to a walk and said, "Have you guys been out exploring?"

"Yeh, Dad!" they replied. "You won't believe what we found on Mole Hill today."

"I was wondering where you've been. I was thinking about having all three of you come with me for a run this evening before we go over to Miss Anne's and Miss Sue's."

"Sorry we missed the run, Dad. But look what we found! And can you guess where we found it?" said Matty. Matty held out the crooked stick to her father as they walked by the lake.

"What a cool snaky-stick, Matty! It's got a nice feel to it," he said. He twirled the stick in his hand the same way Matty had earlier.

"That's not the best part Dad!" said Ryker. "We found it in an old volcano pipe at the top of the hill. You know how you're always telling us it's an extinct volcano . . . well we found an old vent pipe at the top. I suppose I should say Stealth Dog found it. Amos sniffed out the pipe and then dug up this stick."

"*Woo-Hoo*, Stealth Dog!" said their father. "I guess it's a good thing you had him along. That's quite a discovery! Your mom will be excited to hear about it. Speaking of your mom, we'd better high tail it to the house. We don't have long before we leave for dinner. What if I race you two back to the house?"

Before he had finished the sentence they were all running as fast as they could. Their dad liked to win too, but the kids knew he usually held back to make it sporting. Sometimes he would fake a pulled muscle or exhaustion and they'd reach the finish line before he did. Matty and Ryker played along with this, and enjoyed beating him, even if things were rigged.

Stealth Dog pulled into the yard before anyone else and went through his trap door into the kitchen. Ben and Ryker Alder were in a dead heat coming into the yard, with Matty trying to hold them back by their shirt tails. Matty had the crooked stick in her hand, though now the end she was grasping was wrapped up in Mr. Alder's T-shirt. As they approached the enormous sycamore tree that stood in the backyard, Matty yanked back hard on their shirts, pulled her stick free, and went sling-shotting into the lead. Touching the sycamore was the traditional way they finished a race. This time Matty whacked the tree with her stick to win just ahead of her brother and father. "I knew I could beat the men if I just put my brain to it!" she said. Ryker and Mr. Alder looked at each other and both had the same idea. Together they grabbed Matty, pulled her sweatshirt over her head, and rolled her to the ground. The volcano stick went flying in all the confusion.

As they were rolling around wrestling, their mom yelled out to them, "Good win, Matty! Creative use of the shirt tails. You get extra points for that move." Their mom had heard Amos scratching around in his dinner bowl in the kitchen and had come to the mud room door to get everyone moving toward their showers. She said, "That's enough rough-housing! Come on you three, we have to be on the road in 25 minutes. The ladies are expecting us at 7:30."

They all got up from the ground and dashed toward the house. Ryker gave a quick kiss to his mom and kicked off his dirty shoes in the mud room. Mr. Alder tried to give a kiss to his wife. "Ben Alder," said their mom, "you smell like a locker room. I suggest you get showered if you want any attention from me." She shooed Ben on into the mud room. As Matty approached she said, "I forgot something, Mom. I'll be right in." She remembered that the stick and her sweatshirt were lying in the yard. She finally found them in the dim light. She wrapped the stick carefully in the sweatshirt to protect it.

Within 20 minutes they all had cycled through the shower and were finishing dressing. The family knew how to get in and out of baths quickly because they only had one. And the kids had learned to be quick-change artists from their family plays, which they performed at home on Friday nights. When there were too many parts for the four of them to cover, they took turns playing other roles. The trick was to dash behind the folding screen and come out rapidly in new costume. So, getting dressed after a quick bath was a cinch compared to that. Soon everyone was ready and they were off to Miss Anne's and Miss Sue's—everyone except Amos. The children didn't have time to clean him up before they needed to leave. After the afternoon's exploring, Amos was in no condition to take visiting, so he would have to spend the evening guarding the house, and maybe even resting.

It was a fifteen-minute drive to the ladies' house. Matty and Ryker were both lost in thought as they sat in the back of the family car. Their expedition had given them so many things to ponder. Matty had placed the sweatshirt and stick in the trunk of the car. She wanted to show it to Miss Anne and Miss Sue to see what they thought of it.

As they approached the driveway, Beauregard came flying off the porch to greet them. Beauregard was Anne's and Sue's purebred bloodhound, who was also Amos' best-buddy. Anne and Sue heard Beauregard's commotion and came out to greet everyone. Each of the Alders received a hug and kiss from the ladies as they stepped onto the porch of their plantation home.

"Where's our friend Amos?" Miss Sue asked.

"We had to leave him home tonight," Matty answered. "He's pretty dirty from our expedition today."

"Expedition?" said Miss Anne. "Well, you'll have to tell us all about that. Come on inside, everyone."

The ladies escorted them through the front door and into the parlor where a warm fire was burning. Matty and Ryker loved the old house. It had a wooden spiral staircase that curved from the kitchen up to the second floor. The second floor was an assortment of eight oddly shaped rooms of varying sizes. The children loved to hide in these rooms. When they got the chance, they would sneak up the kitchen stairs then whistle for Beauregard. He would bound up the staircase and sniff them out in real blood-hound fashion—they were never able to hide from him for long.

Tonight Beauregard was especially excited to see everyone. It had been a few weeks since the family had come for dinner. The parlor was filled with flowers from the local greenhouse. The ladies loved flowers, and later in the spring and summer they would have plenty from their own garden to fill the house. Matty went over and breathed in the aroma from a large vase full of lily-of-the-valley. The scent was heavenly. Beauregard came to see what all the sniffing was about and put his nose all around Matty, sniffing in and out rapidly. "Beauregard, stop sniffing my pants. I just took a bath," said Matty. Ryker reached over and pulled his tail, and Beauregard spun around to confront his attacker. The energy level started to rise in the room and Ben Alder suggested the kids run on into the kitchen if they wanted to play with the dog. The three of them bounded down the hallway and into the kitchen.

"What a handful we've got! Don't you two agree?" Ben asked.

"Yes, they are," replied Miss Sue, "and we wouldn't have them any other way. Tell me, what have they been up to the past two weeks?"

Mr. and Mrs. Alder looked at one another with wry smiles on their faces. Ben was the first to speak. He said, "Well, they've been busy with school during the week and expeditions on the weekends. Speaking of which, they told me after my run this evening that they'd found something interesting on Mole Hill today. I haven't had a chance to check it out with them, but they think they've found an old vent pipe for the volcano."

Mrs. Alder's eyes got very wide and she said, "Now, Ben Alder, you didn't tell me about *this!*"

"Well I didn't have time, Karen. We had to rush like bandits to get changed for dinner. I forgot about it until just now. I'll admit it sounds a bit suspicious. I'm thinking they probably found some kind of cave made by an underground stream. With all the caverns around here, that seems the most sensible explanation."

"A cavern, eh?" said Anne as she raised her eyebrows. "Well I suppose that could be, but that doesn't sound nearly so intriguing as a volcano pipe when you're nine or ten, now does it?"

"Yes, a volcano pipe beats a cavern any day. I suppose that was my adult imagination trying to explain things realistically," said Mr. Alder.

Just then everyone downstairs heard the repeating sound of a bloodhound's howl. It was a victory howl from the second floor. Matty and Ryker had gone up from the kitchen when Beauregard had started to eat his dinner. After finishing his bowl of scraps, the bloodhound had noticed the kids were missing and went on the hunt.

He finally found them in the closet of an octagonal room on the northeast side of the house. This room was Matty's and Ryker's favorite. It was painted dark green with a hand painted flower border next to the ceiling. All of Miss Anne's and Miss Sue's favorites were represented: polygala, shepherd's purse, aster, swamp rose, wood violets, squaw root, cinquefoil, bellwort, turkey beard, and blue lobelia. The ladies had an artist friend who had painted the border for them. But the best feature of the room was that between the baseboard and chair rail the ladies had covered the walls with pieces of bark they'd picked up in the forest. There were pieces of bark from oaks, tamaracks, pines, sycamores, chestnuts, striped maples, and many other trees. The room gave you the feeling of being right out in the national forest.

When they were discovered, the kids burst out of the closet, knocking over the howling bloodhound as they headed for the back stairs. They spiraled down with Beauregard on their tails, and rushed through the hall to the parlor.

"Hey! Hey! No rough-housing in the parlor. You and Beauregard might break something in here," said Mr. Alder. "You two come over here on the couch and tell the ladies about your discovery today. I started to tell them about it and I realized you haven't told your mother either."

"Our discovery!" said Matty in surprise. "I forgot to get my stick when I saw Beauregard in the driveway. Dad, give me the keys. Miss Anne and Miss Sue, this is going to be really good. You just wait."

Ryker was not one to be left out of story telling. By the time Matty returned, he had recounted the entire afternoon's events to them in short staccato sentences. Miss Anne was especially intrigued and leaned forward as Ryker talked about the stick. As Matty burst into the room carrying her sweatshirt-wrapped prize, Ryker said, "I told them all the good stuff. So just show them the stick."

"Ryker Daniel, I can't believe you! You are nothing but a selfish brat sometimes. You could have waited for me," Matty scolded. "I don't want to show it now."

"But, Matty, I am so interested to see it," coaxed Miss Anne. "Why don't you hold it in your shirt and show all of us. Pretend it's a ceremonial Samurai sword and we're all warriors admiring your skill in wielding it."

Matty couldn't resist a chance to act the part of a Samurai warrior. She slowly bowed from the waist to each person in Japanese style, being careful to keep the stick-sword level in front of her with outstretched arms.

When she got to Miss Anne, she said, "Honorable Master, I present you with the crooked sword of your loyal servant-warrior for inspection." Miss Anne stood up from her chair and bowed from the waist to Matty. She carefully took the sweatshirt and stick in her hands. Her eyebrows rose a few times as she inspected the stick. Gently she handed it back to Matty and said, "Now, honored warrior, keep that sacred tool of honor safe from the elements in its case."

Ryker, who knew he was missing out on some fun acting, finally broke in, "It's just a stick, Miss Anne. Amos found it in the volcano pipe . . . *that's* the interesting part of the story."

"I'm not so sure, my friend," said Miss Anne. "Sue, do you remember that old tale our parents would tell us when we were kids? About the crooked Scottish tree? You remember, the Harry Lauder walking stick tree . . . corkscrew hazel, I think."

"Yes, come to think of it. I remember that now. It had a rhyme that went with it that we learned . . . right?"

"That's right," said Anne. "Let's see if we can remember it." They thought for a long time, exchanging a few ideas back and forth, while the Alders and Beauregard looked around at one another. Finally Anne started the rhyme, and the two of them alternated giving pieces of it until they got out something that went like this:

> From the stump a stem shall grow,
>   Bent like a soul in pain.
> It is a sign of hope reborn,
>   A forest where life seems vain.

> Hold the wand with care ye saints,
>   For it contains the future,
> Of grove and stand and wood alike,
>   In this we must be sure.

"Well," said Anne in a high and drawn out tone, "I think that's it as best as I can recall. Does it sound right to you, Sue?"

Sue said she thought the rhyme was right. They both had been taught the words when they were young. Miss Anne's parents had known Miss Sue's parents before the ladies had been born. Their ancestors had emigrated from Scotland to Virginia in the late 1700's. The old Scottish Presbyterians stuck together closely. They had lots of rhymes and sayings for things in the valley where they lived. Apparently, this was one of the more popular sayings they'd brought with them from Scotland. It had hung on through the generations, strangely enough. Not many families in the valley traced their roots back to 18th century immigrants, so fewer and fewer would have any notion about these sayings.

Matty and Ryker thought this family history stuff was pretty cool. They imagined the original Alders coming over on a ship and setting out through the wilderness. Perhaps they could find out where their family had come from and be able to know their history like Miss Anne and Miss Sue.

The room was quiet for a few minutes while everyone thought about the meaning of the rhyme. Finally Miss Sue said, "Well, I suppose we'd better get on to dinner. You all are probably starving after your exploring."

"And running, too!" piped in Mr. Alder.

Everyone got up to go to the dining room, but Miss Anne hung back and pulled Matty aside. She said, "Matty, be sure to keep that stick wrapped up in its honor cloth unless you are out in the forest somewhere. Take care of it as if it really were a sacred sword."

"Okay, Miss Anne. I'll take good care of it. You can count on me. But what's up with it?" she asked.

"I just can't say, Matty, but I think you've found something special. And we must take care of special things, mustn't we?"

"Yes . . . I guess we should," Matty replied. "And like I said, you can count on me."

As she walked toward the dining room, she thought to herself, *Miss Anne seems awfully strange tonight. I wonder what's going on with her?*

Dinner was a magnificent feast, as usual. Everyone talked about what was on their minds. Matty and Ryker were trying to figure out what new plays to perform. Ryker wanted to do something with King Arthur in it so he could be Merlin. Matty wanted to be Jane Eyre so she could eat cold porridge and practice her pitiful looks. She thought if she got really good at looking pitiful, then it might get her out of school sometime. The adults talked about what was going on in their work and in the community. By 9:30 everyone was getting tired, so they decided to call it a night.

The Alders drove home, each silently pondering the strange rhyme they had heard tonight. Matty especially was trying to piece together its meaning. She wrote the words down when she got home and stayed awake under her covers reviewing them by flashlight. Amos was on the floor next to her bed when she finally fell asleep. The crooked stick was wrapped up in its sweatshirt-case next to Amos. He had one leg resting on it as he lay awake on sentry duty.

HITCHHIKING WITH
MENNONITES

THE SUN WAS SHINING BRIGHTLY through Matty's bedroom window as she woke up. It was a lovely day outside and the cool breezes of the day before had given way to warmer temperatures. Matty lay snuggling under a quilt as warm rays from the sun fell across her bed. When she finally sat up and swung her feet out from under the covers, they came to rest on Amos' back. The sunlight was doing its work on Amos' dark hair and Matty dug her toes around in its warmth.

Sunday mornings in the Alder home were leisurely times for enjoying one another. The family didn't head to church until ten o'clock, so early morning was a time to do whatever they wanted. The house rule was, "You don't have to do anything you don't want to do." There was no schoolwork to be done or workday to get ready for, no soccer game to rush off to, and usually nothing to worry about. Matty especially enjoyed being able to sleep in and bury herself under the covers.

Amos stirred as Matty massaged his back with her toes. He rose up on his rear legs and stretched his paws out as far as they would reach, arching his back in a slow stretch. Then the two friends yawned together, as if on cue. Slowly they picked themselves up, headed into the hallway and down the stairs. The crooked stick, still wrapped in the sweatshirt, was lying on the floor beside the bed.

Mr. and Mrs. Alder were downstairs having coffee in the breakfast nook at the rear of the kitchen. Having finished a game of cribbage, they were starting to read the morning paper as Matty and Amos came in. They laid their papers down, looking up with quizzical grins at two of their sleepyheads.

"Well good morning, Matty! And how's my sleepy boy Amos?" said Mrs. Alder.

"Oh, it's a great day, Mom . . . but we're still trying to wake up. I felt like I could keep snuggling in the sunshine all morning."

"We've been enjoying the sunshine too," said Mr. Alder. "If the weather stays like this, you and Ryker will be planting your garden spot in a couple of weeks. It looks as if the trees will be putting out their flowers and leaves soon."

"Getting the garden in *that* early would be cool, Dad. Which reminds me, I think I'll check on our starter plants in the sunroom."

Matty and Ryker liked to garden. A few years ago their dad had given them a section of their own in the family garden. Now they were in charge of planning what to plant and when to plant it. They had plenty of help from their dad and friends at the garden center. This year they had planted their starters in February. Starting plants early in the year was the key to getting good produce early in the summer; but to do this you needed to have a place to grow plants while it was still cold outside.

Matty, Ryker, and their father grew plants in a sunroom, which was a glass addition on the back of their house. The room was about fifteen feet wide and twenty feet long. Three sides were glass and the other was the wall of the house. The glass on the wall opposite the house curved in a half-arch to form the roof. Mr. Alder and a couple of friends had assembled it from a kit he had purchased at a garden show in the city. A door from the kitchen led right into the room. Entering it was like walking into a miniature nursery. Mr. Alder had tiny tomato, broccoli, and pepper plants growing on shelves. Herbs were placed in pots on the floor where they had been since Mr. Alder brought them in last fall. Mrs. Alder kept different kinds of flowers growing in the room during all but the hottest parts of the year.

Matty and Ryker had a corner of the sunroom in which to grow their favorite plants. Matty had learned very early about plants by growing lima beans. She had started with 10 beans planted in cups of dirt. She let one bean grow to become a plant, but the other nine she dissected one-at-a-time at various stages in their growth. Ever since then she had always had something growing in the sunroom. Ryker learned the lima bean lesson from his sister when he was about four. From then on he too had the gardening bug.

As Matty entered the sunroom on this morning, she saw plants growing everywhere in small pots of different shapes and sizes. She went over to their corner, looked over the plants, watered, and inspected them for disease. They were growing a variety of hot peppers this year, as well as bean plants, and potatoes. She and Ryker tried not to duplicate what their father was growing. The Alders liked lots of variety.

Matty looked up at the sun as she finished tending the plants. It was starting to heat up the room now, and perhaps later they would have to open one of the vent windows. Just then something caught her attention as she turned her eyes from the bright light. Something was scattered all around the big tree in the backyard. She rubbed her eyes to get the blue dots from the bright light to go away. When she opened her eyes again, she saw clearly that sycamore bark was lying everywhere. She yelled for her dad to come and look.

"What's going on, Matty?" he called back from the kitchen.

"Dad! Look! The sycamore tree is losing all its bark."

Mr. Alder got up from the breakfast nook and walked over to the sun room door. He looked out through the glass with some disbelief. To his surprise, he saw bark lying everywhere around the big old sycamore. This was very strange because he had just raked the yard the day before and left it clean. He rushed back into the kitchen, put on his shoes, and went out to investigate. Matty ran out after him in her bare feet and pajamas. They walked around the base of the tree surveying the fallen bark together.

"I'm not sure what to make of it, Matty. Looks like the tree is busting out of its bark."

"It's supposed to peel off some of its bark—right, Dad? Didn't you tell us it doesn't grow like most trees?"

"Yes Matty, it *does* have different bark. It's supposed to be shedding its bark all the time, sort of like a snake shedding its skin, or when a crab molts. Sycamore bark can't stretch as the tree grows like most other species can. Remember, we read that the bark is 'frangible.' The outer layer breaks off slowly in pieces and the layer underneath hardens. That's why the trunk always looks blotchy." Mr. Alder paused a moment then said, "I'm not sure what to make of this. It shouldn't lose the entire outer layer all at once." He walked around the tree, rubbing his chin in his hand. Finally he let out a big sigh and told Matty, "It doesn't look sick to *me*. How about to you?"

"I think it looks pretty healthy, Dad. The new bark seems to be doing okay. It's really smooth."

"Very strange," said Mr. Alder to himself. "We'll have to ask Bob Meyer about this. If anybody will know what's going on, I bet he will."

Bob Meyer was a ranger who worked for the US Forest Service. He went to the Alders' church and had helped them learn most of what they knew about the local forest. "Ranger Bob," as Matty and Ryker called him, accompanied the Alders on family hikes when he wasn't working. Bob was a bachelor who loved children. He especially enjoyed showing Matty and Ryker all the splendid things the forest contained.

Matty was already looking forward to telling Ranger Bob about the sycamore mystery. She thought that since she had discovered the bark, Ryker would have to keep his mouth shut until she had told Ranger Bob the whole story. Thinking about this made Matty wonder where Ryker *was*. No doubt he was still asleep.

They walked back in the kitchen and shared the mystery with Mrs. Alder. Then Matty ran upstairs to tell Ryker what he had been missing. It wasn't long before Matty was gloating over having discovered the sycamore bark and Ryker was rushing downstairs to look things over.

Ryker was mad that he hadn't been first on the scene for the bark-mystery, but he didn't have long to think about it. The Alder's free morning time had quickly passed and the family needed to get ready for church. They cycled through the bathroom and dressed in good clothes, leaving the house a little before ten to drive the short distance to church. The sun was shining even more brightly now, and they were all thinking about the sycamore tree mystery as they pulled into the parking lot.

During the worship service, Mr. and Mrs. Alder tried to focus on the sermon and its message. Ryker occupied himself by taking the pen from the pew rack and sketching on some visitor cards. He drew sycamore trees being exploded by space aliens, large sycamore-eating dinosaurs, and radiation-mutated tree worms that could bore inside a tree trunk and make a sycamore pop like a balloon. Matty thought all of this doodling was quite silly and decided to put a stop to it. She grabbed Ryker's pen away, eliciting a strong frown from her father, which meant she would have to return the pen. She did so, but reluctantly.

Matty was fidgety and kept looking for Ranger Bob. She couldn't see him anywhere and thought he must be working. She glanced round at the people behind her and exchanged stares with other kids. Then she looked at the sun as it came in through the stained glass windows. She watched the colors shift when she moved her head back and forth. One window in particular brought her mind back to the sycamore. This one had a giant tree and a caption underneath that read, "The Tree of Life." Matty knew about this tree from her Sunday school lessons and wondered if it was like her sycamore. She couldn't stop thinking about the sycamore.

When church was over, she and Ryker ran around the crowd trying to find Ranger Bob. Where was he? Mr. and Mrs. Alder got some coffee in the fellowship hall and eased into a conversation with a group of friends. When Matty and Ryker realized that Ranger Bob was nowhere to be found, they ran over and started pulling on their parents' hands to announce they were ready to go home. It seemed to them that Mr. and Mrs. Alder would never stop talking about boring stuff with all those people. Matty and Ryker moved away and started complaining to one another.

"Why do they talk so much, Matty?"

"I don't know. But I wish they would hurry up. I want to get back home and look at the sycamore again."

"Me too. And I've got an idea. What if we rode our bikes over to the ranger's station and found Ranger Bob?"

"What an idea, Ryker! You must getting smarter hanging around with me." She thought for a moment and said, "But if we *do* go out to see Ranger Bob, I get to tell him the story. I saw the tree first . . . even before Dad."

"Yeh, well it was my idea to go find Ranger Bob. So I should get to tell him something."

"Okay, how about this. You tell him we have a great mystery. I'll tell him what I saw. And then you can show him all your drawings from church to see if he thinks any of them are good explanations. How does that sound?"

Matty was thinking to herself that Ryker's drawings were silly and that Ranger Bob would think so too. However, she wanted to be able to tell Ranger Bob the story and thought Ryker would swallow her plan without suspecting anything.

Ryker thought for a moment and said, "It sounds like you get the good part again. But you *did* find the tree, so I guess it will have to do." Matty grinned to herself—her little ruse had worked. In the meantime, Ryker looked around toward his parents and continued, "None of this is going to happen if we don't get Mom and Dad out of here."

The kids went over and started pulling on their parents' arms. Mr. and Mrs. Alder were annoyed by this behavior, but finally relented, said some quick good-byes, and hurried to the car with Matty and Ryker.

"So, what are you both in a rush about?" asked Mrs. Alder.

"Well, Mom," Ryker said in a very nice tone, "Matty and I were thinking we could eat lunch and go out to see Ranger Bob on our bikes. Would that be okay with you?"

"Ben, what do you think?"

"I think that would be fine as long as they take the gravel back road over to the ranger's station. There's hardly any traffic on it."

"All right," answered Mrs. Alder, "but you need to have some lunch first. And you must take Bob some of my apple cake for a snack."

After the Alders arrived at home, they ate a quick lunch of grilled tuna sandwiches, potato chips, and some fruit salad. The kids then rushed to get ready for their adventure. They put on some play clothes, got water bottles and a snack together, packed these in a couple of backpacks along with the apple cake, and headed to the garage to get their bikes. Amos saw all the planning and decided he wasn't going to be left behind. He followed them outside.

Ryker was getting on his bike as Matty hesitated at the door. He whined, "Let's go, Matty."

"Just a minute. I forgot the crooked stick. I want to show it to Ranger Bob."

"Well hurry up. We've got to get going."

Matty rushed back into the house and up to her room. Amos was on her heels the entire way. She grabbed the crooked stick, which was still in its sweatshirt case.

This won't do for an adventure, she thought to herself. She looked around the room to find a better case to keep the stick in. Finally, she found just the right thing: an old clarinet case her mom had sewn for her. She slid one end of the stick into the cloth clarinet bag while she held the opening firmly. Then she shook the stick down into the bag and put the whole thing into her backpack, leaving about a third of the bag poking out through the zipper at the top. Matty shouldered the backpack and adjusted the straps until it was comfortable.

The next instant she and Amos were running back to the garage where Ryker was becoming quite impatient. As soon as he saw Matty come through the backdoor, Ryker started peddling and Amos bolted down the driveway after him. Matty got to the garage, jumped on her bike, and wheeled down the driveway after her brother and Amos. The three friends were on their way to the ranger's station.

It took them about half an hour to bicycle to the station. They didn't have to pull off the gravel road for any cars. The only people they passed were Old Order Mennonites in their horse-drawn buggies heading towards town. There was a large community of Mennonites in the county. They lived much like the Pennsylvania Amish. Matty and Ryker thought it strange that they wore black clothes and never drove cars. Amos didn't pay much attention to the people, but loved the horses—getting very excited whenever he saw one. Matty had decided that, "Amos just thinks the horses are big dogs that want to play with him."

When Matty and Ryker finally arrived at the ranger's station, they left their bikes by a large hemlock tree out front. The station building was a large split-log building, stained a dark brown with a green cedar shake roof. They went up on the porch and tried the door. It was locked, so they looked in through the window to see if anyone was around. Ranger Bob was nowhere to be seen. Matty and Ryker decided he was out checking campsites or fishing permits. His big dark-green, four-wheel-drive truck was not at the station. They decided to wait a while for Ranger Bob and eat their snacks at the picnic area behind the station.

About a quarter mile from the back door of the station a stream ran through the forest. Next to the stream the Forest Service had constructed a small picnic area. A washed gravel path led through thick mountain laurels down a small grade to the picnic area. The kids carried their backpacks down the hill to the stream. Before eating, they splashed their hands about in the water, tossed rocks, and tried to get Amos to go swimming. The air was very warm for springtime, but the mountain fed stream still had the feel of icy cold winter. Amos waded in up to his knees and decided that was enough for him.

Soon play gave way to hunger and the kids broke out their snacks. Matty had remembered to bring dog biscuits and a rawhide bone, so even Amos had something to eat. After an unhurried meal and with their stomachs full, they relaxed for a nap like the one they'd taken the day before on Mole Hill.

Not long after they'd fallen asleep, they heard the sound of a truck on the road. *Ranger Bob's,* they thought. The laurels were so thick they couldn't see the station or the road. Matty and Ryker got their things together and headed up the hill. As they walked, they heard the truck stop and after a few moments, tear off down the gravel road. They wondered, *Why would Ranger Bob be speeding away so quickly?*

Matty and Ryker hiked up to the station porch but couldn't see Ranger Bob's truck anywhere. A dust cloud lay heavy on the road in the direction they had traveled from town. The dust was settling in the other direction toward a small lake where people often fished.

"Well, it looks like Ranger Bob must have taken off again, Ryker. I think we'd better head toward home. It's no telling how long he will be this time."

"I don't want to go without telling him, Matty!" Ryker pouted.

"We'll find him sometime, Ryker. And besides, it's not you that gets to tell him. Remember?"

With that announcement Matty headed over toward the hemlock tree to get her bike. Ryker followed her, wanting to catch up and argue the point more.

"Where's my bike, Ryker?" Matty said as she looked toward the hemlock.

"Where's *your* bike? You mean, where's *my* bike? I left it right here next to yours."

Both bikes had disappeared. Amos walked around the tree sniffing vigorously. The hair on his back bristled at what he smelled. He began to growl and look down the road toward the settling dust. Something was certainly amiss.

"Can you believe it, Ryker? I think somebody has stolen our bikes. Look at Amos. He's picked up somebody's smell. And he doesn't like it!"

"Nobody steals anything around here, Matty," Ryker said in disbelief. "Mom and Dad even leave the keys in the car."

"Well something's been stolen now. And that means we're left without a ride."

"How are we going to get home?" Ryker whined.

"I suppose we can stay here crying about it or we can do something," said Matty.

After some brainstorming, the kids ruled out breaking into the office or setting a signal fire. Both of these would get them into *big* trouble, so they decided to start walking back to town instead. They hoped Ranger Bob would drive by and give them a lift. It seemed like a long way home on foot.

"Amos walked all the way out here. If he can do it," said Ryker, "we can too."

"That's the Alder spirit," said Matty. "And we'd better not pass whoever stole our bikes, or Amos will chew 'em to pieces." Matty turned and growled at Amos. Amos instinctively looked down the road and growled in the direction the truck had gone.

Their fighting words had set their spirits high, and the three friends set off on foot. After 35 minutes of steady walking, they made it to their turnoff. There was still no sign of Ranger Bob, which sorely disappointed them. The road onto which they turned was the same road on which they had seen all the Mennonite buggies earlier. It was more heavily traveled than the ranger's station road. Perhaps they could flag down another person they knew and get a ride.

They walked down the road toward town for what seemed like hours. Matty and Ryker were exhausted, and it was getting late in the afternoon. Amos was the real trooper in the bunch, staying alert and leading them on. After trudging along a bit more, Matty noticed that Amos had stopped about halfway up a hill they were climbing. His ears were standing up, listening. Matty halted, and the crunching sound of gravel beneath her shoes stopped. Ryker pulled up behind her. In the quiet she could make out the sound of a horse's hooves and buggy wheels approaching from the far side of the hill, but the buggy was still hidden from view on the other side of the hill's crest. The sound got louder and finally a flatbed buggy, pulled by a large thoroughbred horse came over the hilltop. It was coming down the middle of the road toward them. The kids stepped off to the side. Amos stood in the middle of the road to meet the big "dog" pulling the buggy. The Mennonite husband and wife saw Matty and Ryker and the man stopped the flatbed next to them.

"Hello, children," said the woman, "where are you heading so late in the afternoon?"

"We're walking back to town," said Matty. "Somebody stole our bikes out by the ranger's station."

"Things just aren't right when people will steal your bicycle out in the country," said the man.

"I'm Amelia Horst and this is my husband Nelson," the woman said nodding toward the man. "We live on a dairy farm just down the road. If you came from the ranger's station, you must have passed it," said Mrs. Horst.

"Is it the big one with the greeting sign at the entrance?" asked Matty.

Mr. Horst replied "Yes, that's the one. It says, 'If you don't have time to stop . . . '"

"'. . . then smile as you drive by!'" Ryker burst in.

"That's it exactly!" Mrs. Horst smiled and said.

The friends had certainly noticed the Horst's dairy farm as they passed it. Behind the welcome sign, the fields were colored a lush green from the early rye and barley crops. The Horst's neatly kept white farmhouse had made the kids long to be home, where they could get a meal and bath.

"I wanted to stop," Ryker said sulking. "Matty thought your driveway was too long to take a detour on. So, we kept walking."

"Seems like we'd better give you a lift back into town before your parents start worrying about you. What are your names? And, where do you live?"

"I'm Ryker Alder. This is Matty, my sister. And that's Famous Amos, our dog."

"'Famous Amos?' That's an unusual name for a dog. What's he famous for?" asked Mr. Horst.

"He's brave and fearless and once he saved us from a bear. He could probably eat up your whole horse if he needed to," Ryker exclaimed.

"Well, we'd better not have that happening right now or none of us will get home tonight. Besides, it seems he and old Dunlap are making friends," said Mrs. Horst.

Sure enough, Amos had been sniffing Dunlap's hooves and the old horse had bent his head down to see what was going on. They were now nose to nose and licking at one another.

"Come on, Ryker, Matty, and Amos Alder. Hop On! Our buggy is yours to ride on," said Mrs. Horst.

The three friends piled on the back of the flatbed buggy. Amos ran in circles on the wooden floorboards barking wildly with excitement. The kids dangled their feet off the back of the flatbed while Mr. Horst turned the buggy around toward town. Soon the kids were bumping along in the wagon with a good breeze at their backs. They were looking back at the road over which they'd traveled so long, and Matty and Ryker were both glad to be finished with the long hike. Dunlap was moving the buggy along at a good pace.

"This sure beats walking," Ryker breathed aloud to Matty.

Matty nodded to her brother, then took off her backpack and brought it around to her chest. She pulled it close against her and felt the crooked stick that was inside and then eased the case out of the backpack. She wanted to feel the stick against her hand. There was some comfort in knowing that her crooked Samurai-sword stick hadn't been stolen along with her bike. She gently slipped the stick from its case and felt it in her hands. She waved it back and forth in the breeze over the gravel road behind them in sword-like motions.

Ryker was watching what he thought were pathetic attempts by his sister at swordplay. He'd show her what real swordplay looked like. He wrenched the stick from Matty, bent over, and hit the gravel road with it. Matty put her backpack down and grabbed her brother's shirt, trying to get the stick back.

Ryker struggled against his sister and said, "Just watch me for awhile. I'll show you how to use a sword."

Every five or ten feet he would strike the ground with the stick saying things like, "Take *that*, evil Knight! I, Arthur of Camelot, will not yield to you." All the while Matty was fussing at him and attempting to wrestle the stick out of his hands. The struggle for control of the stick went on for more than a minute. They were getting close to the edge of town and Ryker gave the road one last stroke that was so hard Matty thought it would break the stick. Then he sat up, raised the stick aloft, and said, "I knight thee Sir Sissy Pants," and whacked Matty's shoulder with the stick.

Matty was furious with how Ryker was handling her precious stick, so she punched him in the stomach and grabbed wildly to get it back. But as they tussled, Amos pushed between them to look at something behind the wagon. Matty turned to see what had caught Amos' attention and she screamed out, "Look!"

Ryker turned to look, still keeping a firm grasp on the stick. In the middle of the road they had just passed over was a five foot high Fraser fir tree. It hadn't been there before.

DISCOVERING THE MAGIC

AFTER MATTY SCREAMED, she and Ryker were frozen,
trying to figure out how the tree had appeared in the
middle of the road. The Horsts, who'd been alarmed by
Matty's high voice, turned around to find out what was
going on. The buggy, meanwhile, was quickly cresting
another hill. With their attention on Matty and her alarm,
the Horsts didn't notice the fir tree before it slipped out of
sight.

Matty felt their eyes on her. She couldn't say anything
about the tree. What could she say? She imagined herself
saying, "Hey, did you see that tree pop up out of
nowhere?" It just seemed too ridiculous. Matty paused a
moment. No! She definitely couldn't say that. They'd

think she was crazy. And anyway, she didn't know what to think about the tree herself.

Ryker, on the other hand, was ready to blurt out everything to the Horsts. Matty saw this and gave him her sternest glare to shut him up. Such glares often had the opposite effect on Ryker, making him do exactly what Matty didn't want him to do. But Ryker was also unsure about what he'd seen. Had his eyes deceived him? Matty's glare was enough to help him hold his tongue.

Mrs. Horst finally asked what was wrong, and for some reason, which even later that evening when reflecting on the situation Matty wouldn't understand, she lied. She told Mrs. Horst a spider had been crawling up her pants and she was sorry her scream had scared them.

"That's all right, Dear . . . spiders are enough to scare anyone," Mrs. Horst replied.

She and Mr. Horst turned back around, and they continued heading for the Alder home. Matty grabbed the crooked stick out of Ryker's hands, quickly put it in its case and put her backpack on again.

She and Ryker were nearly silent the rest of the way home. Matty was preoccupied, asking herself, "Where did that lie come from," until Ryker interrupted the silence. He started to ask, "Did you see . . . ;" but Matty cut him off mid-sentence and put her finger to her lips. She wanted him to zip his mouth until they got home.

It was dinner time when the buggy pulled into the Alder residence. Matty, Ryker, and Amos jumped down off the back of the buggy with their gear. Mr. and Mrs.

Alder came out of the house to see who had come to visit. It wasn't every day they had a buggy pull up in the drive-way. The Horsts got down and introduced themselves to the Alders, told them where they lived, and relayed their part of the afternoon's story. The Alders listened, staring wild-eyed at their children.

The Alders and Horsts talked for some time about a few disturbing things happening in their peaceful county. In the course of talking, they discovered they had mutual friends in Miss Anne and Miss Sue. Mrs. Horst often worked with the ladies in the local disaster relief efforts, and Miss Anne was even planning to visit their farm on Thursday. The two couples talked about the current relief projects for some time, then Mr. Horst told everyone they would have to be going because it would soon be time to milk their dairy cows. The Alders thanked the Horsts for taking care of their children. Mr. and Mrs. Horst said they were pleased to be able to help, and that the three friends were quite charming. As they got back onto their buggy to leave, Mrs. Horst told Ryker and Matty to stop by the dairy farm sometime for some fresh milk. Ryker promised if they couldn't stop, they'd at least "smile as they went by." Everyone laughed together at this reminder of the sign in front of the farm. Then Mr. Horst shook the reins to get Dunlap moving toward home. The Alders went inside the house and got ready for their Sunday evening meal together.

Over dinner Matty and Ryker told their version of the afternoon's events. They recounted how they couldn't find

Ranger Bob, how their bikes had been stolen, and how they had met the Horsts on the long trek home. Matty and Ryker still kept quiet about the fir tree. They wanted to finish dinner and talk things over between themselves. Both wondered what explanation the other had to offer about the tree's appearing out of nowhere. Dinner finally ended. After Matty and Ryker finished cleaning up the dishes, they ran upstairs into Matty's room with Amos following.

Matty jumped onto her bed, put a pillow on the far side that was next to the wall, turned and sat cross-legged facing Ryker. Ryker pulled up Matty's large blue bean-bag chair, plopped down in it, and kicked his heels up onto the edge of the bed. Amos laid himself down at Ryker's side and closed his eyes.

"Finally Ryker, we have some time to piece this together. I can't believe what I saw today—but you saw it, too. Now, why don't *you* tell *me* what you saw, and we'll go from there."

"What do you mean, '*You* tell *me* what you saw?' Why don't *you* tell *me* what *you* saw?"

"Ryker why are you being so difficult? You always want to tell everything before me. So, go ahead."

"Noooo!" he said mockingly. "I insist. Ladies first."

"OOOHHH, Ryker Daniel. You can be so exasperating," Matty said in a fluster. "You know very well what I saw. It was the same thing you saw. We both saw a tree appear out of nowhere. Like magic! And all you want to do is be a big brat right now!"

The tension in the room was rising. Ryker snapped back, "I'm not a big brat. *You're* the brat. I don't like you telling me what to do all the time." Ryker looked around with some satisfaction at having said this. Then he said in an uppity voice, "I saw a tree . . . and for your information it was a *Fraser* fir. Just like the Christmas tree we cut down at the tree farm. So *there*."

"I remember what a Fraser fir tree looks like, Ryker," Matty growled. She was getting tired of arguing. Finally she barked out loudly, "Now, *where* do you think it came from?" As she said this, she pulled her hair on both sides of her head, and as she finished speaking let out a growl. Amos sat up on his hind legs and looked at them both.

Ryker knew right away Matty was reaching her meltdown point. He realized he was being difficult for no good reason. Why was he so grumpy? He didn't know. After Matty's growl he was silent for a few moments, and decided to quit being difficult. He wanted to be a little nicer to Matty, so he said softly, "All right, Matty. I guess I *am* being a big brat. I don't know what to make of the tree. And, I'm not sure why I feel like fighting. I'm all mixed up. I'm really mad about our bikes. I sure wish Amos and I could get our hands on those thieves. We'd tear them up." He growled at Amos and bared his teeth. Amos looked at Matty as if to ask, "What is wrong with *him*?"

Matty glanced at Amos and then said to Ryker, "I'm angry about the bikes too, Ryker . . . just let's not take it out on each other. Thanks for apologizing. Now, let's put our heads together on this tree thing. There has to be some kind of explanation."

Ryker thought for a moment and said, "It seems lots of strange stuff has been happening since we found that crooked stick in the volcano vent."

Matty thought for a moment. "That reminds me, Ryker. Miss Anne said something to me last night about the stick. She seemed pretty strange when she said it. She told me there was something special about the stick and to take really good care of it."

"Matty!" Ryker exclaimed. "Do you remember what I did just before we saw the tree pop up? I was playing King Arthur and I hit the road really hard with the stick." As Ryker said this, he got up on his knees in the bean bag and swung his arms around to demonstrate the sword play motions.

"That's right," Matty yelled. "And do you remember what I did with it last night when we finished our race with Dad?" Matty moved to the edge of her bed as she said this. Amos perked up both ears.

"No, what'd you do?" asked Ryker.

"I hit the sycamore with the stick. And it was popping out of its skin this morning."

"Do you think they're connected, Matty?"

"You know what Dad tells us about problem solving: The *key* is to experiment."

"That's great, Sis. We should devise an experiment to test our hypothesis." Ryker stopped and looked a little puzzled. "Matty? What is our hypothesis?"

Matty replied, "That somehow, Ryker, my friend, the two stick-striking incidents are connected with the strange occurrences."

"Yes, that's our hypothesis," Ryker said definitely. "We'll need to recreate the original conditions as closely as possible in order to test the hypothesis. It's elementary my dear Watson . . . El-e-men-tar-y!" he said, drawing out the syllables of the last word.

Ryker and Matty loved playing Sherlock Holmes and Dr. Watson. The family often read together the adventures of the great detective. They had even acted out some of the stories in family skits. Here was a mystery that needed Holmes and Watson. And the three friends knew how to play the parts. Ryker would be Holmes, Matty, Dr. Watson, and Amos, one of Holmes' Baker Street boys, who always gathered the best intelligence information. A perfect job for Stealth Dog.

"Okay, Holmes, we need to get to work. We'll have to be in bed before long, so we need to hurry."

"We don't have to go to bed early tonight. Did you forget, Watson my man? It's spring break this week. We've got the whole week off."

"What luck, Holmes! Get your Baker Street Boy on the job. I'm off on a lead."

With this Matty jumped from the bed and went downstairs to retrieve the crooked stick she'd left in the mud room. Ryker started to fill Amos in on the mystery. As Matty went through the kitchen, she passed her mom and dad, who were enjoying a cup of tea together.

"Hey, young lady, where are you heading in such a hurry?" asked Mrs. Alder.

"Holmes and I are off to check a hypothesis, my good woman."

"Well, tell Holmes and his Baker Street Boy that you can't leave the yard. We've had enough excitement for one day," said Mrs. Alder.

"What's the hypothesis, Watson?" asked Mr. Alder.

Ryker and Amos entered the kitchen just then. Ryker replied, "We can't discuss that with just anyone, you know. You'll have to wait until Watson writes it up for the papers, my good man."

"All right, Mr. Holmes, we'll wait to read tomorrow's edition of the *Strand*. But don't you and Watson forget, you still need to be in bed tonight—even if you have the week off. Remember that you have an invitation from Mr. Showalter for tomorrow morning," said Mr. Alder.

"*Gadzooks*, Holmes! I'd almost forgotten that invitation. We must hurry," said Matty.

"Not a problem, my good Watson. And now, the game is afoot."

Ryker sped into the closet in the front room to get the Holmes and Watson outfits from the family costume box. Matty ran on into the mud room to get the stick. The three friends met up in the hallway, put on their sleuth getups, and ran into the backyard with the crooked stick.

The stars were shining brightly in the evening sky along with a gibbous moon. It was still unusually warm following the summer-like day. When they got to the back yard, Matty looked up and saw the constellation Orion in the western sky. "Look Ryker, there's Orion the Hunter. He's hunting for something, just like us."

"No," Ryker said condescendingly, "he's hunting. We're fooling around looking at the stars. Come on, Matty. Let's get started in the garage."

They ran to the garage, which was at the end of the driveway past the big sycamore. Ryker went in, turned on the overhead lights and the lights on his father's workbench. The workbench was at the back of the garage in front of their parents' cars. Matty followed Ryker up to the workbench and pulled the crooked stick from its case.

"Where should we begin, Watson?"

"Remember what you said, Holmes. 'Recreate the conditions.'" Matty thought for a moment. "We have two different mysteries. The first one was when you whacked the road with the stick. The second was when I whacked the sycamore tree. So, we need to duplicate those as nearly as we can."

"Right, Watson. Here, I'll take the stick and duplicate my mystery."

Ryker picked up the stick from the workbench and swung it around in the air. Matty wondered what Ryker was trying to do. She and Amos stepped back to avoid Ryker's wild strokes. Ryker repeated his King Arthur words about the evil knight and then slammed the stick down onto the garage floor. No sparks flew. No fir tree appeared. Nothing happened.

"Well, Watson, no trees growing here," and Ryker pointed to the spot where he'd struck the ground.

"What *are* you, brain damaged, Ryker? Of course there's not going to be any tree growing there. It's solid concrete. Do you think a tree can grow in concrete?"

"Quit calling me names, Watson. Remember you're just my helper in these mysteries. I'm playing Holmes."

"Maybe I should be Holmes this time. Come on, we need to find some dirt."

Matty took the stick from Ryker and went out into the gravel driveway. Ryker and Amos followed her. She was looking around for a good spot to try her experiment. She decided to test her hypothesis on the far side of the garage, out of sight of the house. In the strong moonlight, she raised the stick over her head and brought it down hard on the ground. She turned her head as the stick hit the dirt and quickly stepped backward, as if expecting an explosion. As she turned back around, Matty's jaw dropped open. In the dim light she could see a small seedling rising where she'd struck the ground. "Ryker! Look!" she screamed with excitement. She bent down to see what the tree was like and to watch it growing. It was like one of those movies made with stop-motion photography. They'd seen a movie like that in school which showed how a plant grew from a seed to full height.

As Matty was examining the tree, Ryker said, "Watson, you've done it. Now let *Sherlock Holmes* give it a try."

Ryker took the stick from Matty and started striking the ground here and there. Matty finally looked away from the growing tree and saw what Ryker was doing.

"Ryker, stop! What are you doing? How are we going to explain all these trees to Mom and Dad in the morning? Give me that stick!" And she took the stick from him and ran back into the garage to put it in its case. Amos followed her.

There were now half a dozen seedlings growing near the garage. Ryker was examining them in the moonlight when the floodlights on the corner of the garage flicked on. Matty had turned on the lights so they could get a better look at the tree she'd helped to create. She and Amos came back around the corner of the garage with the stick, now back in its case. The three friends could see the new seedlings growing slowly but surely in the electric light. Matty's was the tallest tree now. She thought the tree was some kind of birch because it had rough papery bark. She couldn't tell what species the other trees were. None of them had any leaves yet.

The three friends watched the trees for about five minutes. Amos chose one of Ryker's trees to mark. "Amos, quit peeing on my trees," Ryker scolded.

"He's a dog, Ryker. What do you expect him to do? Just leave him alone," Matty scolded back.

After a few more minutes of examining and sniffing, it was clear to everyone that the growth of the trees was slowing down. The trees were at various heights and diameters now. The tallest was one of Ryker's saplings, which was about three-feet tall and an inch in diameter.

"I can't see them growing at all anymore, Matty. Why do you think they've stopped? The fir tree was at least five-feet tall."

"Ryker, these trees are all different kinds. The stick doesn't seem to grow just fir trees. And in real life fir trees grow a lot faster than birches do; so maybe my birch tree just can't grow as fast as a fir."

"Brilliant, Watson. I'm glad I suggested you get up to speed on trees."

Matty rolled her eyes and turned away from him. She took the stick out of its case again. Then she brought her arm behind her to swing the stick. Ryker asked, "What are you doing now, Watson?"

"I'm testing our other hypothesis, Holmes. Do I have to do all the brain-work?" And with this Matty smartly swung the crooked stick against her birch tree. They didn't notice any spectacular change. Matty put the stick back in its case and they waited. They watched. Something was happening. The birch bark was peeling back. Ryker swore the tree was getting taller and ran into the garage to get a tape measure. Before he returned, Matty noticed that small peels of birch bark were falling to the ground.

"I'm going to measure this tree," Ryker said when he got back. "Then we'll measure it again in a couple of minutes."

"I know it's growing Ryker. Pieces of bark have been falling off while you were in the garage."

"I want to be exact, Watson. So, here goes." Ryker took a measurement of the birch tree and stood back to watch. Amos had gotten tired of all the tree business and gone off toward the house. Matty bent down and picked up some birch bark to examine. As she stood back up, they heard their father's voice calling from the mud room door.

"Holmes and Watson, your Baker Street Boy is over here wanting to come in. Somebody locked his trap door. I suggest you both retire for the night along with him. You have a big day ahead of you tomorrow with Mr. Showalter."

"Okay, Dad, we'll be back in a couple of minutes," Matty yelled back.

Matty stood there thinking for a moment. Ryker was busily measuring the birch tree. "It *is* bigger Matty. It's grown two inches since I measured it."

"I know it's growing Ryker. I *told* you to look at the bark," Matty said in irritation. "And, we've got to do something about this little tree patch. If Mom and Dad come out in the morning and see all these trees, they won't know what to think."

Matty didn't know why, but she didn't want to tell her parents what the stick could do. Not just yet. So, she decided that she and Ryker would get rid of all the saplings before they went to bed.

"Ryker, we have to pull up all these trees before we go in. If Mom and Dad see them in the morning, they'll have a cow. I don't want them to know about the stick yet."

"Pull them all up? But they just started growing. You'll kill them."

"We don't have to kill them Ryker. We'll pull them up, set them in a water bucket overnight, and the replant them somewhere else later. Okay?"

"All right. As long as we don't have to kill them. But just think, Matty. We could make gazillions of dollars with this stick. If we whacked our starter plants, do you think they'd grow bigger?"

"I don't know," Matty said, still quite annoyed. "Will you get those dollar signs out of your head and get to work finding us a water bucket. I'll start pulling up the trees."

It was tough work pulling up the birch tree, which was the biggest at this point. The smaller saplings came out of the ground pretty easily. When they were all uprooted, Matty smoothed the gravel and dirt as best she could to make everything look normal. Meanwhile, Ryker had gone into the garage and filled a five gallon bucket with water. He returned to tell Matty that he couldn't carry the bucket alone, so together they dragged the bucket around to the back wall of the garage. Then they placed the uprooted trees in the water and were done with the hard work. But now they needed to come up with a cover story for their parents about their Holmes and Watson adventure. They told them they had been chasing evil Moriarty, who wanted to overthrow the world using mind-altering jelly beans. Their parents were quite impressed with the evilness of Moriarty's plan. They told Holmes and Watson they were grateful that they'd saved the world, but even sleuths had to be in bed soon. Matty and Ryker took off their costumes and headed upstairs for quick baths before getting under the covers.

TREES FROM MIDAIR

IT WAS BRIGHT AND BEAUTIFUL on Monday morning. Ben and Karen Alder were having their coffee and listening to the weather report when Matty came through the kitchen. The radio weatherman was predicting that the entire week would be warm and sunny. This was great luck because the entire family had outdoor plans this week. Mr. and Mrs. Alder were both taking time off from work to be with the children during spring break.

The night before, Matty had determined to wake up earlier than her parents in order to fix any remaining damage to the driveway. There might be holes or dirt left behind from their experiments. Her determination was not, however, enough to overcome her need for a long, deep sleep. The previous day's adventures had "flat worn her out," as people in their community would say. She slept through her alarm and woke much later than she had planned. Luckily, since her parents weren't going to work today, they hadn't ventured out to the garage.

As Matty began to leave the kitchen quietly, she heard the beginning of a strange report on the news. The reporter was talking about a series of trees that had been mysteriously planted in the middle of Route 259. *That was the road where the Horsts picked us up yesterday,* Matty thought as she listened. The reporter said local officials were trying to understand why anyone would have planted trees in the roadway. "One of the trees, a Fraser fir, was approximately eight feet in height. Fortunately, the trees were reported to the authorities before they caused any accidents. Road crews removed the trees, and officials are investigating the matter," announced the reporter.

At the end of the report, Mr. Alder turned to Matty and said, "That was the road you were on last night, wasn't it Matty? Did you see anything out of the ordinary?"

Matty was thinking about those "officials." What if they found out about the stick? They'd surely take it away from her and Ryker. So she answered, "No Dad, I would remember seeing an *eight*-foot tree in the road." She emphasized the word "eight." She'd only seen a five-foot tree, so it didn't seem like a real lie to her. She quickly hurried out of the kitchen after answering her dad's question and went through the mud room to the back yard.

Matty walked across the yard toward the garage. The sky was a reddish purply blue this morning. A few wispy high clouds were floating northward over the Alder home. Matty crossed the yard heading toward the garage. As she got closer, her heart started to race. There were lines of tiny saplings curving around all over the place. They criss-crossed and figure-eighted on the driveway and went around the corner of the garage. Two lines ran out from the side door of the garage.

Where did these come from? Matty thought in panic. She went to the garage door and started pulling the tiny trees up in handfuls. They were about twelve- to fourteen-inches tall and spaced fairly evenly.

"We didn't hit the ground in all these places," Matty thought as she worked. "What happened?" She went on her hands and knees across the driveway pulling up saplings. She moved around to the other side of the garage and pulled them up there.

"I don't understand this," she said in exasperation.

Finally, when they were all uprooted, she dumped the small saplings on the compost pile at the edge of the property. She ran to the garage, retrieved a gravel rake, and smoothed out the driveway. She was finally finished. If it hadn't been for the new trees, she wouldn't have had any work to do that morning. They'd done a good job of cleaning up from the bigger sapling uprootings the night before. Now that everything looked close to normal, she went behind the garage to inspect the big trees. The half-dozen saplings filled the five gallon plastic bucket, which

Ryker had placed next to the back wall of the garage. All of the young trees seemed to be doing well in their temporary water bath. From her experience with other plants, Matty knew the trees would last a while in the bucket. Before too much time went by she and Ryker would find a home for them.

When Matty returned to the house, her mom asked her to go and wake Ryker. Mrs. Alder said she would have their breakfast ready in a few minutes: pancakes, bacon, and eggs. "You'll both need a hearty breakfast to get you through until our picnic with the Showalters," she said, reminding Matty of their date.

"Mr. Showalter? I almost forgot, Mom! I'll be back with Ryker in a jiff." She ran upstairs, petted Amos, who was lying on his side in the middle of the hallway, shook Ryker awake, and reminded him they had to be at Mr. Showalter's hangar by 10 A.M.

"Mom's got breakfast ready, so get downstairs and eat. You can put your clothes on in a minute," Matty said rushing out of the room.

Ryker threw off the covers, excited for the day ahead. *A ride in a biplane*, he thought gleefully. *I bet no other kid in school has ever ridden in an open biplane.*

Karen Alder and Mary Showalter had first met while serving meals at the local soup kitchen, and had become fast friends. Mary and her husband John owned the local aerial spraying service. She ran the office, while John and two other pilots did the spraying. The Showalters had never had children of their own, and instantly fell in love with the Alder children the first time they met them.

The two ladies had arranged a few weeks ago for Mr. Showalter to take the children flying today—weather permitting. Besides the planes used for spraying, Mr. Showalter owned an old biplane he'd restored a few years ago. The ladies knew it would thrill the kids to fly in it. But since the biplane had open cockpits, the weather needed to be warm and clear. Today fit the bill perfectly.

The kids finished their breakfast in a hurry and ran upstairs to get ready. Mr. Alder went up to oversee the preparations. The kids needed to take their long under-wear, ski hats with the facemasks, gloves, and overcoats. Mr. Alder wanted them to have anything they would need with them. He didn't know how cold it would be flying in the open cockpit. *Better to have everything in the trunk*, he thought. As Matty was getting her gear together, she decided to bring the crooked stick along. After losing her bicycle yesterday, she wasn't taking any chances with thieves.

Matty's and Ryker's parents were accompanying them to the airfield. Mrs. Showalter would give them a tour of their facilities while the kids were off flying. Amos was invited for the tour too. Afterwards, everyone was going down to the river to enjoy a picnic lunch.

By 9:30 the family had their gear and picnic basket packed in the car. When they'd made a final run through their checklist of things-to-take, they headed to the air-field.

Mr. Showalter had the dark blue biplane rolled out in front of the hangar when the Alders drove up. Mr. Alder parked their car in front of the office, which was at the side of a large airplane hangar. As soon as the car stopped, Ryker burst from the back seat and ran full-speed to the biplane with Amos chasing after him. Mr. Showalter smiled as he saw them coming.

"Are you ready for takeoff, Captain Ryker? And how about your friend?"

"Yes Sir, Colonel Showalter. I'm ready for action, but my friend is stuck on ground patrol. Will we be taking on the Red Baron this morning?"

"No, not just yet. First, we need to get you checked out on the new top secret equipment. After that, you'll be cleared to go gunning for the Baron."

"Yes Sir." Ryker saluted. "Whatever you say, Colonel."

By this time the rest of the family had made their way to the plane to look it over.

"Quite a beautiful piece of machinery, John," said Mrs. Alder.

"It sure is," added Mr. Alder.

Mr. Showalter smiled with pride and said, "It took a lot of hours to get her into this kind of condition. She's my pride and joy." He turned toward the kids and said, "I've been looking forward to taking you two up in her. Mrs. Showalter's been on me to get you both up in the air. Looks like the weather's going to cooperate today. Let's go and see what Mary's doing in the office."

They made their way over to the office door and the Alders followed Mr. Showalter in. Amos waited outside near the door. Mrs. Showalter was busy with her regular office work. She was trying to get some papers filed before the Alders arrived. When the folks came in, she stopped what she was doing.

"Ben! Karen! Ryker! Matty!" She said each name slowly, lingering on it, and then hugged that person. This was how she always greeted them, and it made each of them feel important. "Now, where's my other boy?" she asked.

"We left him outside, Mary," Mrs. Alder told her.

"Now, you just bring him on in. He's one of the family too." Everyone grinned, and Mr. Alder walked to the door and let Amos in. Mrs. Showalter greeted Amos just as she had the others, saying his name slowly and hugging his neck. Then she gave him a biscuit. When she'd finished with Amos she turned to the kids saying, "Are you two ready for your plane ride?"

"You bet," they replied.

"John, you better take them with you and run them through the checklist." Mrs. Showalter turned her attention back to the kids and said, "Any pilot of ours has to know how to do a proper equipment inspection."

"I'll get them up to speed, General Showalter. They're good recruits," Mr. Showalter assured his wife. "Come on, you two. Let's get that bird ready to fly."

Mr. Showalter left the office with Matty, Ryker, and Amos in tow. He walked back to the plane and worked through the preflight checklist a second time for the benefit of the children. Mr. and Mrs. Alder sat down to chat with Mrs. Showalter, while the inspection was being performed. After fifteen minutes or so, the plane was ready to get airborne.

Mr. and Mrs. Alder wandered out to the plane with Mrs. Showalter as Mr. Showalter was helping the children select the right type of clothing to wear from the assortment they'd brought with them. When they'd selected the right items, Mr. Showalter went into the hangar to put on his gear, while the other adults helped the kids get bundled up for the flight. It took some time to get Matty and Ryker suited up, making sure everything was tucked in and covered properly.

Mr. Showalter returned in time to watch the last of the preparations and to give his approval to everything. When all was complete, he turned to the other adults to discuss the flight plan for the day. Matty seized the opportunity to run to the car and get her crooked stick. She snuck it under her coat to have it near her, and then returned to the plane.

Since leaving the office, Amos had spent most of his time lying under the plane in the shade. The sun was high in the morning sky. The air was warm at ground-level and windless—perfect for their early spring flight. The two pilots who worked for the Showalters came out of the hangar and helped the kids into the front compartment of the biplane. The stick made it awkward for Matty to raise her leg over the edge, so one of the men, not knowing what the trouble was, picked her up and set her down in the backseat. She let the stick slide from underneath her coat onto the floor as she sat down.

There were two mini-seats in the compartment, one behind the other, separated by a removable backrest. After Ryker hopped into the forward seat, the men strapped in both kids. Next they put helmets on the kids that had goggles and intercoms attached to them. They showed Matty and Ryker the intercom switches, which would allow them to talk to one another or to Mr. Showalter.

Mr. Showalter climbed in the rear compartment and put on his helmet. He turned on the intercom and asked, "Are you ready?" Matty toggled her switch and said, "Yes Sir!"

"Are we all clear out there?" he asked his men.

"One second," said Mr. Alder, who called Amos out from under the plane. Everyone stepped back a good distance. One of the men gave Mr. Showalter a thumbs-up. He started the plane and smoke rumbled from the open exhaust pipes. Soon the engine revved up to a loud steady roar. As he throttled up the engine, Matty and Ryker waved to their parents. The biplane taxied out to the runway, Mr. Showalter put the throttle down, and in seconds they were lifting into the air. They flew up over the treetops past the end of the runway, and Matty looked back to see their parents still waving at them. Amos was barking excitedly in the plane's direction.

Mr. Showalter flew Matty and Ryker over town to start. They spotted their school and church, the town square, and grocery store. Soon Mr. Showalter made a pass over the Alders' home. Matty and Ryker both thought their house looked small from the air. As they hung their heads over the side of the plane, the rushing wind was cold, even with helmets and winter gear on. Mr. Showalter asked over the intercom if they had had enough. Ryker flicked the switch, turned around and yelled, "No way! This is too cool. Keep going!" Matty felt the same way. *What a blast!* she thought.

Mr. Showalter banked the plane westward toward the National Forest. The air was crisp and exhilarating, rushing across the children's faces. Matty and Ryker saw below them the road they had traveled with the Horsts, and they were able to pick out the Horst's dairy farm as they flew over. They waved, even though they knew the Horsts couldn't see them. Ryker made a big cheesy grin toward Matty and then turned it toward the ground, remembering his promise to Mr. Horst to smile when he went by. He and Matty giggled hilariously at this. Matty flicked on the intercom and said, "Ryker, you just did a fly-by smiling." They giggled even more. Mr. Showalter had seen the Horst's sign when driving to the forest, and finally figured out what the kids had done. He too broke out in a loud chuckle, which only he could hear.

They turned south over the Horst property, circled, and headed west toward the National Forest again. The Horst's fields were freshly plowed and ready for the spring planting. From the air it looked as if someone had pulled a comb across the land. Matty noticed a farmer plowing his fields on the property next to the Horst's. The plane was flying high now and the tractor looked like a toy. Matty looked back at Mr. Showalter and pointed down at the farmer. Mr. Showalter saw the tractor and banked the plane downward in a hard left-hand turn. He wanted to give Matty a closer look.

Matty reached down and grabbed her stick during the steep turn. She opened the top of the case and clutched the smooth wood tightly in her hand, which made her feel safer. The plane turned downward and leveled out at about 400 feet. Mr. Showalter had sprayed these fields once and knew the man on the tractor was Mr. Arborcide. He buzzed around the field and tractor a number of times. Ryker held his head over the side for a good look. Matty, still a little queasy from the steep descent, held firmly onto the stick for comfort. After a couple more passes, which got the attention of Mr. Arborcide, Mr. Showalter slowly turned toward the forest. With the plane level, Matty relaxed and packed the stick back away in her coat.

They flew over Ranger Bob's station, which was north of Mr. Arborcide's farm. Then they flew by the lake that lay north of the station. Flying on, they saw the mountain cliffs on which one could find climbers practicing their skills every weekend. The steep walls looked so tiny to Matty and Ryker from the airplane. They had hiked on the ridge above these cliffs and knew how high they really were. What a thrill it was to see them from above!

They flew northwest over the forest another half hour, seeing places they'd never been. Mr. Showalter knew many of the peaks by name and introduced the kids to them. They were having a ball, but it was time now to get back. Mr. Showalter turned the plane southeast toward the airfield. Another thirty minutes and they'd be there. That half-hour went by faster than any Matty and Ryker had ever spent. As they touched down, Matty and Ryker wanted nothing more than to keep flying.

They slowly taxied off the runway, and Amos ran out to provide a barking escort for the plane on its approach to the hangar. Mr. Showalter's men were waiting to chock the plane's wheels and help the three of them out of their harnesses. When Ryker was unhooked, he jumped to the ground, ran to his mom and dad, and said, "I want to take flying lessons!"

Mrs. Showalter laughed good humouredly, and said, "Sweetie, you *will* be a pilot. I'd bet on it; but you'll have to wait just a *few* more years before John can start giving you lessons."

Everyone laughed at this, and Matty said, "Ryker, you are so silly."

"I'm not silly," he said looking around. "I *will* be a pilot. I'll show you."

Mrs. Alder didn't want the fun of the day to be spoiled by a fight, so she said, "You two go and get out of those winter clothes. We've got a picnic to get on with down by the river."

The kids hurried over to the car and shed their winter garb. They were becoming hot as they stood in the spring sunshine. They placed everything in the trunk and Matty made sure to hide the crooked stick away underneath everything. Meanwhile, Mr. Showalter walked over to the hangar and took off his heavily-lined flight suit. When he had stripped down to his everyday work clothes, he looked at the thermometer inside the hangar. It was 70 degrees now in the shade. He walked back toward the biplane. Matty and Ryker had already returned, and were standing with the Alders and Mrs. Showalter. Mr. Showalter said to everyone, "Talk about global warming! Seventy degrees in the shade already! It sure got warm while we were up flying!"

Mr. Alder responded, "Yes, it's warming up fast this morning and it's only barely spring. I hope this isn't a sign of what the summer will be like."

Mrs. Showalter chided, "Now you boys quit talking about the weather, and start *doing* something about getting us something to eat. Let's get on down to that shady spot by the river."

Mr. Showalter told his two pilots where they'd be if anything important came up, and asked them to watch the office. The gang then piled into Mr. Showalter's big 4x4 vehicle and headed to the river to eat. The food in the picnic baskets smelled wonderful to everyone. The baskets held cold fried chicken, fruit-filled Jell-O salads, potato salad, fresh bread, cupcakes, and dog treats.

Everyone was hungry from their morning activities. When they arrived at the picnic spot along the river, the men spread a couple of checkered blankets on the grass under a large beech tree. Everyone took a seat on the blankets, except Amos, who sat in the grass. After a quick prayer by Mrs. Showalter, everyone dug into the food.

They'd been eating a little while when Mr. Showalter remembered that the cooler full of drinks was still in the 4x4. They'd all been so famished they'd forgotten about drinking. But when Mr. Showalter reminded them about the cooler, everyone felt parched to the bone. Ryker went with Mr. Showalter to the 4x4 where they retrieved the cooler and then returned to the picnic. They passed out Cokes and juices to everyone. The Coke tasted especially good to Ryker, who chugged his down and promptly got out another. After he guzzled down the second, Mrs. Alder noticed the two empty cans and scolded, "No more sodas, young man."

Everyone filled up on the great food, but not so much that they couldn't enjoy the chocolate cupcakes. Ryker ate his cupcake quickly, just like he'd drunk his Cokes. Matty slowly ate the icing off her cupcake, then slowly ate the cake. She then let Amos lick the sticky, sweet residue from her fingers. Amos took his time and removed every bit of icing. While all the licking was going on, Ryker climbed up in the beech tree. The tree was full of good climbing branches and Matty followed her brother when Amos was finished licking her fingers.

Mr. Alder laid his head in his wife's lap so he could watch his children climbing through the tree above them. Mr. Showalter talked about what they'd seen on the flight that day: the town, the Alder home, the Horst farm, the tractor and farmer, Bob Meyer's station, and the forest.

Mr. Showalter's words about seeing the Horst farm reminded Mr. Alder about the news report earlier in the day. The Showalters hadn't heard about the strange trees in the road near the Horst's. They listened attentively to the details Ben Alder gave. Ryker hadn't heard the report about the trees in the roadway and looked at Matty questioningly. She wrinkled her brow and shook her head to signal him not to ask about it right now.

"Strange things are going on with trees around here," said Mr. Showalter. "Bob Meyer asked me to keep my eyes peeled for odd stuff when I'm spraying the National Forest parcels for gypsy moths. But he didn't say what kind of 'stuff' I'm supposed to look for. I'm bettin' he'd say those trees are 'odd stuff.'"

"Speaking of the forest, did we tell you the kids had their bikes stolen out by the ranger's station yesterday?" Mrs. Alder asked with a furrowed brow. As the kids listened, they remembered their anger over the theft of their bicycles.

"My lands, what is this county coming to?" Mrs. Showalter said anxiously.

"I don't know sometimes, Mary," Mr. Alder said. He paused a moment, looking up at the kids, and said to Mr. Showalter, "You know, John, we're going hiking tomorrow with Bob in the National Forest. I'll ask him what he thinks of those trees out on 259."

Ryker again looked at Matty in wonder about the trees. Reluctantly, she leaned over and whispered in his ear, "We need to talk about this later. Not in front of Mom and Dad."

Mr. Alder was looking up and asked, "What are you two whispering about? I hope you aren't thinking of throwing things on us?"

"Now that you mention it, Dad, . . ." said Matty as she pulled off Ryker's shoe and dropped it on Mr. Alder.

"Whew!" exclaimed Mr. Showalter. "They're throwing stink bombs at us. We'd better clear out of here."

The adults got up laughing and headed to the river to look things over. Amos led the way down and jumped in to cool off. Ryker, irritated about his shoe, pushed Matty off her branch. She dropped the short distance to the ground, hit the picnic blanket running, and caught up with the adults. Ryker swung to the ground, grabbed his shoe, and hopped one-footed toward the others until he could get his shoe on.

After a leisurely stroll along the river, the picnickers decided it was time to get back to the airfield. They packed up the baskets, folded the checkered blankets, and put things in the 4x4. Mr. Showalter gave Ryker a towel to dry off Amos. When Ryker had finished wiping down the dog's fur, everyone climbed into the truck, and Mr. Showalter headed it back toward the airfield.

As they pulled onto the airfield road, Mr. Showalter noticed an unfamiliar truck parked in front of the office. "Looks like we've got customers today," he said. The "customer" turned out to be an old man, who was arguing with the two pilots in front of the hangar. By the way he was flailing his arms and yelling, the Alders and Showalters could see he was very agitated.

"You know who that is, Mary? It's old man Arborcide. I flew the kids around his place a few times this morning. We waved and I thought he waved back. I wonder what he's all steamed about."

"I don't know John," said Mrs. Showalter, "but you better get to him before he riles one of the men."

Mr. Showalter parked the 4x4 in front of the office and headed over to talk with Mr. Arborcide. He sent his men off to do some other work, and got Arborcide to step into the hangar out of the sun. The old man proceeded to yell at Mr. Showalter about something.

Mrs. Showalter felt embarrassed by the scene Mr. Arborcide was making, so she asked the Alders to come into the office. "It's a bit cooler inside. Let's go relax for a minute." Everyone walked toward the office, but as they approached the door, Matty and Ryker begged to go over and look at the biplane instead of going inside. Mrs. Showalter acquiesced, but asked the children to stay out of Mr. Showalter's way. Matty and Ryker ran from the office to the biplane, started circling and touching it from the nose to tail. Amos, meanwhile, was sniffing around the strange truck. The hair on his back was bristling.

From the plane, Matty overheard Mr. Arborcide yelling something about trees in his field. Ryker heard it too and they looked at one another. The temptation was too great for them, and they snuck to the door of the hangar and listened. Amos followed along, his hair still standing on end.

"I don't know what you're talking about Mr. Arborcide. How could I plant saplings from midair? That plane's not even equipped for spraying, much less planting. It's a show plane," Mr. Showalter said with a note of irritation in his voice.

"Well those trees weren't there until you'd been buzzin' my fields," shot back Mr. Arborcide.

"This is just ludicrous, Arborcide. I couldn't plant trees from 400 feet in the air. And if I'd spread seed, do you really think it could have sprouted in two hours?" Mr. Showalter snapped back in disbelief.

"I knows what I seen: you flying over my place and a couple hours later I've got these dang trees in my newly plowed field. My boys has got to waste their time pulling them up by hand. We can't leave them there. They'd make a mess of my equipment come harvest time."

"Mr. Arborcide, all we did was wave to you. I had a couple of kids with me on a sightseeing flight."

Just then Ryker bumped into the chain on the hangar door. Mr. Arborcide turned around and saw the kids and Amos. "Who are *you?*" he asked gruffly.

"I'm Ryker Alder. Who are *you?*" Ryker answered defiantly.

Matty grabbed Ryker's shoulder and said, "Mind your manners, Ryker." She looked at Mr. Arborcide and said sweetly, "We're Ben and Karen Alder's kids. We live out on the edge of town."

"I know you," said Arborcide with his face scrunched up. "Your Pa's that crazy man runs around with a flashing light on."

"He's not crazy. *You're* crazy," Ryker yelled in defense of his dad.

"Tell *me* he's not crazy? I nearly wrecked my truck one day trying to avoid hitting the darned fool."

Ryker's blood was boiling now. He yelled out, "You're a mean old man." Amos' hair was standing all the way on end now, and he was growling a low threatening growl at the man.

"Arborcide, I think it's time you left. You came to say your piece, and you've said it. I'm not involved with those trees in your field. So, you better look some other place for answers," barked Mr. Showalter, cutting off the conversation. He went over to escort Mr. Arborcide to his truck.

Arborcide turned and said, "I can find my *own* way out!" He turned to Matty and Ryker as he was leaving and said, "I'll be keeping my eye on the two of you . . . and on that flea bag mutt too. Kids these days ain't got no manners. You just proved my point about your father." With this he headed toward the truck.

This last comment was too much for even Matty to take. She yelled after him, "You *are* a mean old man, Mr. Arborcide," and started to cry. Amos knew the man had hurt Matty somehow. He ran after him, teeth bared. Mr.

Showalter called Amos to stop. Arborcide turned and saw Amos, started running, and made it to his truck just in time to miss being jumped on. He yelled some more at the dog, started his truck, and left in a hurry. Amos held his ground barking.

Mr. Showalter stooped down as Amos was chasing Mr. Arborcide into his truck and picked up Matty. He hugged her and said, "There, there, Matty. I'm so sorry you were here when that happened. He *is* a mean old man. And he sounds a little crazy to me. Imagine, you and me planting seedlings in his field from 400 feet up. Doesn't that sound crazy to you? Don't take any of what he said to heart."

Matty stopped crying when Mr. Showalter mentioned the seedlings. As she hugged him, she looked at Ryker over his shoulder. Ryker saw that she had something to tell him. Matty hadn't talked to Ryker about the seedlings she'd found in the driveway and yard earlier in the day. They must be connected with Mr. Arborcide's seedlings. She had carried the stick with her in the plane. But how could the stick plant trees from 400 feet in the air? The mystery would have to wait to be solved until they were alone again.

The other adults came out to see what Amos was barking at. Mr. Showalter took the kids over toward the office and informed their parents about the incident. Mr. Alder was inwardly proud of how the kids had stuck up for him. The story made him remember almost being hit by Mr. Arborcide. He told everyone about it. Mr. Arborcide's truck, loaded down with logs was coming up a hill toward

Mr. Alder. Mr. Alder was running against traffic as usual. When a car came from the opposite direction, there was no room for the truck to swing wide since Mr. Alder was on the shoulder. It seems Mr. Arborcide didn't want to lose his momentum on the hill, so he just kept coming at Mr. Alder. Mr. Alder finally had to jump off the road's shoulder into the drainage ditch to avoid being hit by the truck. Somebody in the passenger's seat had yelled and shaken their fist at Mr. Alder.

"That would have been one of Arborcide's sons: Chop or Buzz. They're rough ones from what I hear," said Mr. Showalter.

"Ben, you never told me about that," said Mrs. Alder.

"I didn't want you to worry, Honey. It's the only time it's happened to me around here," he replied.

"Next time you need to tell me about this kind of thing. We don't keep secrets from each other," said Mrs. Alder. Matty and Ryker looked at one another.

"Well that just goes to show you. Arborcide is just a mean and crazy old man," said Mrs. Showalter. This comment seemed so out of character for mild-mannered Mary, that everyone started to laugh—even Ryker, whose temper was cooling down now.

When the laughing died down Mrs. Alder said, "We'd better get home, everyone. Kids, what do you say to the Showalters?"

The kids thanked the couple over and over again. What a morning it had been! They walked to the Alders' car together. Mr. Showalter apologized again for not keeping the kids away from Arborcide. The Alders told him that he'd not done anything he needed to be sorry for. It was Mr. Arborcide who needed to apologize, and the Alders were going to keep their eye on him.

A DAY IN THE NATIONAL FOREST

THE FOLLOWING MORNING the Alders were all waiting on their front porch dressed in hiking gear: cotton pants, leather boots, floppy hats, water bottles, binoculars, backpacks, and walking sticks. Matty and Ryker were rocking in the front porch swing, which hung on chains from the ceiling. Mr. and Mrs. Alder were sitting on the glider bench holding hands. A truck carrying cows for the live-stock auction was passing by when the cordless phone rang. Mrs. Alder picked it up from the table next to the glider, "Hello? . . . Why, hello Bob. . . . We're just waiting for you out on the porch. . . . No, we're not in a big hurry today. . . . Oh, I think the kids would love to help with that. . . . The real question is: Are you sure we won't get in the way? . . . All right, if you think it will work. . . . We'll be ready when you get here."

She turned off the phone, placed it back on the table, and filled in the rest of the family. "That was Bob. He's going to be late. It seems the other rangers were called to a big meeting, so his boss needs him to get a few things done today. He was wondering if we would mind helping him do some work while we hiked. I told him that would be fine."

"Ranger's work?" Ryker asked. "If so, I'm the man for the job. What does he need? To trap a black bear or catch some poachers? How about tagging some deer?"

"No. I don't think those things were on the list," Mrs. Alder replied with a smile. "Taking a few soil samples and posting new trail markers are what I recall him mentioning. But if any bears or poachers *are* around, I'm sure you're the man he'd want at his side." Mrs. Alder loved to see Ryker's boldness and daring. Sometimes this side of him could be challenging to deal with, but she tried her best not to squelch this strength of his.

"When is he coming, Mom?" asked Matty.

"He has to pick up some soil kits and trail markers, before he heads over. I'd say he'll be another thirty to forty-five minutes."

"Is it all right if we go and play for awhile?" asked Matty.

"That's fine, but stay in the yard," Mrs. Alder told her. "I want to be able to find you when Bob gets here."

"Okay, Mom." And turning to Ryker she said, "Come on, let's go to the garage. I need to show you something."

Matty jumped over the porch railing onto the ground, then dashed off toward the garage with Ryker following quickly behind. Amos, who had been lying next to the glider asleep, heard the commotion, thought something big was going on, and leaped over the railing running. The three stopped at the far side of the garage, where the tree experiments had been performed on Sunday evening. Matty took off her backpack with the crooked stick poking out from the top. Ryker stripped off his backpack too and put it down next to the side of the garage. Amos looked around, and seemed a bit disappointed at having been awakened from a good nap for no more action than this. He laid himself down to wait for more interesting developments.

"What are we doing out here, Matty?"

"Ryker, we need to talk," she said deliberately. "Yesterday, we didn't have time to figure out where those trees in the field came from. Remember?"

"I totally forgot about those trees. I mean we went to the mall and the movies after the plane ride. . . . And that was cool—that slimy green monster eating dogs and people. I've got to be a special effects engineer someday."

"Ryker, can you stay on one subject at a time? I forgot about the trees in Mr. Arborcide's field too, but when Mom started talking about the soil test, I remembered I'd forgotten to tell you there were seedlings all around the garage yesterday when I got up. They were about three inches high and were in lines that curved everywhere."

"How could you forget to tell me something like *that?*" Ryker blurted.

Matty started to defend herself, "Well, I didn't see *you* helping me clean them up, Mr. Sleep-in-Bed-All-Day." She gave him a huge glare, then continued, "And besides, I got caught up getting ready for our plane ride. I put them all on the compost pile. It's got to be connected to that stuff with Mr. Arborcide. When we flew around his property, I had the stick with me."

"You had the stick with you while we were *flying?*" Ryker was incredulous.

Again Matty defended herself. "I didn't want anybody to steal the stick from the house, so I took it with me. Then I got scared when we did that big dive toward Mr. Arborcide's, and I unwrapped the stick and held really tight. It made me feel safe having it in my hand."

"Big Dive? *That* wasn't a big dive. Boy, you're a wimp."

"Ryker, are you going to be difficult again today?" Matty growled.

Ryker rolled his eyes and said, "I am *not* difficult. Besides, tell me what it is we're doing out here?"

"I think the seedlings next to the garage and the ones in Mr. Arborcide's field are connected. We need to do another experiment with the stick . . . something like our lima bean experiment . . . to see how and when the stick makes trees grow."

Ryker agreed that more experiments were in order. Something about experimentation really thrilled him, so he said, "All right. Why don't we try something over by the compost pile, where you threw the other trees?"

"That's the spirit! *Now* you're not being difficult. I'll bring the stick."

Matty picked up her backpack and headed toward the compost pile. Amos and Ryker followed. When she arrived, she took the stick, which was still in its case, out of the backpack. She said, "Ryker, we didn't hit the ground in all those places where I pulled up the seedlings. And we were 400 feet above Mr. Arborcide's field. That can only mean one thing. The stick can also work without hitting something."

"That makes sense to me. Give it here. I've got just the experiment."

Matty stepped back from him and said, "No way. You're always swinging it around. This calls for a woman's touch."

"Then I better go get Mom," Ryker quipped, then laughed.

Matty ignored this and slid the case halfway off the stick, without touching the wood. She held one end of it using the case as a glove and then struck the ground very hard with the exposed end. Nothing happened. She tried it again, swinging harder this time. Amos, hearing the stick *swoosh* through the air, backed away from Matty. There was a crack on the ground where the stick hit, but still nothing unusual.

"Ryker? Did you see that? Nothing happened. No tree."

"Let me have it. I'll get it to work." Ryker grabbed the bare end of the stick, drew it from the case and out of Matty's grasp. He struck the compost pile hard. Instantly a black locust tree sprouted up on the pile, and soon topped out at three-feet high.

"See?" Ryker said shrugging his shoulders, as if to convince Matty that *he* knew how to run an experiment. "It still works. Look at that locust tree I just made."

"Ryker, now I *know* you're brain damaged! You're missing the whole point. Of course the stick works. Don't you get it? You're touching it. Hold it with your hat and try that again."

Ryker pulled off his floppy cap, grabbed the end of the stick using it like a glove, and struck the compost again. Nothing happened this time.

"See?" Matty said, nodding her head downward with raised eyebrows. "Nothing. It's just like I was thinking. If you're touching the stick, *that's* what makes it work. And we already know it works better the harder you hit something."

"I don't understand," Ryker said, now becoming frustrated that he wasn't following things.

"It's got to be touching someone's skin to work, Ryker. That's what the experiment proves. And when you add what happened to Mr. Arborcide's field, *and* the lines of seedlings near the garage, there's only one conclusion. The stick can grow trees whenever it's in your hand."

"But it didn't grow any trees in the garage," Ryker countered.

"That's because the garage floor is concrete. Let's do another experiment. Let's get some of those patio stones behind the garage and bring them down here." They went over, picked up two of the paving stones, and set them down near the compost pile.

Matty said, "Before we do the next experiment, you need to pull up that tree and stick it in the bucket with the others. It won't do to have a tree in the compost pile."

Ryker pulled up the locust tree and ran it over to the bucket. When he got back, Matty was ready to continue.

She said, "Now take the stick in your hand, drag it through the compost and over the stones."

Ryker took the stick and did as Matty asked. He stepped back. Matty took the stick from him, holding it by the case. Amos moved forward and sniffed at the line in the dirt. They watched a couple of minutes.

"Look, Ryker. Do you see those small sprouts?"

Small trees were slowly sprouting up along the dirt line Ryker had drawn. Ryker was getting it now. He said, "There aren't any on the patio stones. I get it. You have to have the stick in your hand *and* it has to be touching some dirt."

"Yes, but that's not all. Remember the plane. It doesn't have to touch the dirt. One more experiment, now. Take the stick and draw a line parallel to that one, but keep the stick up in the air."

Ryker took the stick in his hand again. He slowly moved it in a line parallel to the last one he'd drawn in the dirt, this time holding the stick a few inches above the ground. He stepped back. Matty took the stick and put it back in the case."

"Nothing's happening, Matty."

"It will. I'll bet my allowance on it. We didn't see those seedlings next to the garage until the morning after our experiments. I think it just takes a little longer to grow them this way."

As she was saying this, Ranger Bob drove up the road in his green Forest Service truck. It was a large new SUV with a National Forest Service emblem on the door, and was equipped with police lights, a siren, and a large shallow metal basket on the roof for carrying equipment. His turn signal was on, and he was slowing to turn into the driveway. "Come on! Ranger Bob's here. We'll have to let this experiment keep cooking for now." And the three friends ran off to greet their friend.

Bob parked his truck in the driveway and walked toward the porch. The kids and Amos flew around the corner of the garage bearing down on Ranger Bob. He turned just in time to meet their oncoming tackle. Bob was a very big man. "Built solid—like a tank," people would often say of him. The kids and Amos loved nothing better than wrestling with this big man, who was like a teddy bear to them. Bob squared himself to meet the tackle. The three friends hit him mid-thigh at full speed. Their combined weight didn't budge the ranger. He toppled them to the ground and jumped on top of them. Amos alone managed to escape.

Mr. and Mrs. Alder watched the attempted tackle and wrestling match that followed. Bob held the kids down, tickling them relentlessly for a couple of minutes. Matty and Ryker kept yelling between giggles that they couldn't take any more. Amos was running around playfully nipping at Bob and pulling his pants from behind. Bob told the kids they had to say "Uncle," if they wanted mercy—to which they both said, "No way." More tickling ensued, followed by Ryker's yelling out, "George!"

Ranger Bob said, "George? You've got to say 'uncle.'" He tickled him some more.

"But George *is* my uncle," Ryker giggled.

"You know what I mean," Bob chuckled back.

Ryker finally relented, saying, "Uncle." Matty gave in as well and Bob picked the kids up, one under each arm, and walked them toward the porch.

"Hello, Ben. Hello, Karen. I found these bandits running amok on your place. You want me to lock 'em up?"

"No, I have a better idea," Mrs. Alder answered. "How about making them put in a few hours of community service in the National Forest?"

The kids, dangling under Ranger Bob's arms, squeaked out, "We'll do the forest work. Pleeeeeeease, not the lock up."

"Seems too good for scoundrels who'd try and tackle a defenseless man," said Bob.

Ryker squeaked again, this time in disbelief, "Defenseless?"

Bob gave his dangling quarry a little shake, accompanied by some more rib tickling, and said, "Like I told you, a DE-FENSE-LESS man like me. Well Karen, if community service is the punishment, then I'll enforce it." Ranger Bob put the kids down, ruffled the hair on their heads, then said, "Are you two ready to get to work in the forest? And let's not forget that backbiting fuzzy-tailed accomplice of yours." Amos perked up his ears and looked at Bob.

Ryker yelled out, "We sure are. Let's go."

"Ryker, we forgot our backpacks. They're behind the garage," said Matty as she ran off to retrieve her backpack and stick. Ryker and Amos followed her to the garage again.

Bob Meyer walked over to the porch and asked the Alders, "How'd you two get so lucky to have these kids?"

"Don't know, Bob. Must be doing something right though," said Mr. Alder. "Here they come again. What are they dragging with them now?"

While they were getting their backpacks, Matty had seen the bucket of trees and thought, *Ranger Bob could tell us what kinds of trees these are.* She hoped this might tell her a little more about the stick. They'd need to explain where the trees had come from, so she and Ryker agreed to say they'd gotten them from a friend. It took all their strength to carry the bucket around the garage. The adults watched them come across the driveway, all four hands on the handle of the bucket, struggling against its weight. The saplings were bouncing up and down, while water splashed onto the ground.

"What do you have now?" asked Mrs. Alder.

Matty told her, "They're trees Mom. We're replanting them for a friend. He didn't have room to plant them at his house."

"And we need Ranger Bob to help us identify them," Ryker added.

Bob walked over and gave them a hand getting the bucket to the yard. Mr. and Mrs. Alder came down off the porch to look at the bucket full of trees. The water was thick and brown, but offered glimpses of the mass of tangled roots underneath its surface. Ranger Bob helped the kids set the bucket down in the grass and started fingering the saplings one at a time, examining them closely with a scientist's eye.

"Hey Bob, are you finally putting those degrees in forestry and dendrology to good work?" Mr. Alder asked teasingly.

Bob wasn't paying attention. He was studying the trees with a puzzled look on his face. After a few moments he said, "Tell me where you got all these trees again?"

"A friend's dad didn't want them on his property, and gave 'em to us to replant," Matty told him.

Bob looked even more puzzled, and said, "All these trees from one piece of property? Are you sure?" Matty and Ryker were starting to feel cornered in their cover story. They were fumbling around for an answer when Mr. Alder asked, "What's got you all perplexed about this bucket of trees, Bob?" asked Mrs. Alder.

"Well, this is quite a variety of trees to have in one place. You've got a cucumber magnolia. Find 'em mostly on hillsides around here. This one's a cottonwood . . . likes wet soil. This looks like a black locust. Pretty common. Now, this one . . . hmmm . . . is a slippery elm. You find them on the moist valley floors usually. Then we've got a striped maple. Pesky things are taking over the forest floor around here. This is a yellow birch, and then this last one's a dogwood." He handled each tree as he talked about it.

"That *is* quite a variety." said Mrs. Alder. "Who gave these to you, kids?"

Ryker looked at Matty. She hesitated, then turned and said to her mother, "It was Timmy Johnson's dad. Timmy is in my class at school and lives on a farm across town. Mr. Johnson must have dropped them off while we were at Mr. Showalter's yesterday." Matty looked back at Ryker wondering if the story was flying with the adults.

"Hmmm," Bob sighed, still pondering the variety of trees. After thinking he said, "They all look healthy. I suppose we could plant them today in the forest. They're all native species in this area, and our hike will take us through some diverse habitats." Bob looked over to Mrs. Alder and said, "I'm guessing you don't want all these growing on your place."

"I think the forest is the *perfect* spot for them Bob," Mrs. Alder replied quickly. "We can help you plant them today." She thought her family already had more plants than they could deal with. The sunroom was full and the garden soon would be.

Bob smiled at Mrs. Alder and said, "Great! We'll load them on the roof rack of the truck and take them with us. We just need some old feed sacks or something. We'll wet the sacks and wrap the roots to keep them from drying out as we drive."

Matty and Ryker were relieved that the cover story was working. Not wanting any further questions, they dashed off to the garage to get some old towels the family kept in their rag bag. They soaked a few towels with the garden hose and ran back with them. Bob was taking the saplings out of the water and laying them on the ground in pairs when they returned. He put the striped maple to the side and said, "The forest is overrun with these maples as it is. They're crowding out the slower growing seedlings. So, I'm not going to replant this one. We can either plant it here, or put it on the compost pile."

"Put it back in the bucket, Bob. The kids can take care of it later," Mr. Alder said.

Bob put the maple into the bucket, took the towels from Matty and Ryker, and wrapped the roots of the other trees with them. Then he picked up the saplings, stepped up on the bumper of the truck, and placed the trees down in the roof rack. He used two tie-down straps to secure them.

As Bob was stepping down off the truck, Mr. Alder asked him, "Say Bob, all these trees made me remember something. We've got a couple of tree mysteries to ask you about." Mr. Alder told Bob about the sycamore tree and the incident with Mr. Arborcide. Bob Meyer listened with his eyes scrunched up as if puzzling through something.

"Well the Arborcide thing sounds a lot like what happened out on 259. Did you hear about those trees?" Matty and Ryker looked at one another.

Mr. Alder said, "Yes, we heard about it on the radio. What do you make of it?"

"The sheriff thinks somebody was playing a prank, from what I hear. Hard to imagine how somebody would be able to plant seedlings on Arborcide's place during broad daylight, though. I'm not sure what to make of it. He lives out on 259 though." Bob scratched his head and continued, "About your sycamore. I can't say as I've heard anything like that before. Let's have a look at it."

Bob and Mr. and Mrs. Alder walked over and looked at the sycamore tree together. Matty, Ryker, and Amos stayed near the truck. The children, worried they might get in trouble for the trees and seedlings that had appeared. They started to plan ways to avoid the trouble. However, their parents didn't spend much time looking over the sycamore with Ranger Bob. The kids stopped talking when the adults turned back their way. They over-heard Bob tell their mom and dad, "I don't know what to make of your sycamore mystery. It's a real puzzler."

The adults walked back quietly toward the big Forest Service truck and the children. When they stopped, Mr. Alder piped up quizzically, "Seems healthy enough, Bob. The sycamore, that is. It's just strange . . . that's all."

"I'll ask a couple of the other rangers to see if they might know what happened. Right now, I suppose we'd better get going. We've got a lot of work *and fun* to get accomplished today," the big ranger said. Matty and Ryker were relieved that Ranger Bob and their parents weren't asking any more questions.

The Alders picked up their hiking gear, loaded into the big truck with Bob, and drove off in the direction of the National Forest. Ryker and Matty were in the front seat next to their friend, while Mr. and Mrs. Alder along with Amos were in the back seat being chauffeured.

It took them about thirty minutes to reach the isolated section of the forest where Ranger Bob wanted to go hiking. The trailhead was north of the ranger's station in an area not much used by the public. The rangers were hoping to encourage more hiking in this part of the forest. So today Bob's assignment was to nail yellow, diamond markers on a five-mile section of trail. Along the way he would collect soil samples as part of an ongoing impact study the Forest Service was conducting. If more people started   using the area, the soil samples would help the rangers understand how the land was being impacted.

Bob pulled the truck off the main road onto a rugged fire access road that led to the trailhead. He asked Ryker to engage the four-wheel drive by pulling back on the lever between his feet. A wide grin broke on Ryker's face and he looked up at Ranger Bob to make sure he'd heard him correctly. Bob smiled and nodded to him. Ryker gave the lever a hard tug and the truck jerked into four-wheel drive. Bob eased the truck forward along the bumpy road and in a few minutes they came to a metal gate blocking their path.

"Here's where we get out and hoof it," Bob told the Alders.

Everyone climbed down out of the truck. The Alders put on backpacks and picked up their walking sticks while Bob got the saplings and a fold-up fire shovel down from the roof of the truck. Bob strapped the shovel on top of his backpack, which contained his lunch, drinking water, soil sampling kits, trail markers, nails, tool pouch, and hammer. He put on his pack, hoisted half the trees on one shoulder, and gave the others to Mr. Alder to carry. Then they hiked down the access road about 300 feet to the trailhead. Bob stopped and took the hammer, nails, trail markers, and empty tool pouch out of his backpack. He put the trail marking equipment in the pouch and strapped it on. A large shagbark hickory stood at the head of the trail. Bob nailed the first marker to the tree, then picked up the saplings he'd laid down on the road. He started up the trail and everyone followed except for Amos, who took the lead, vigorously sniffing the trees and rocks beside the trail.

The trail was rugged, but a forest crew had done some clearing and leveling recently to make it more accessible to the public. Since the leaves were only just starting to fill out, there was plenty of sunshine on the forest floor. Bob nailed up markers every 100-150 feet or wherever people might miss the direction the trail was taking. Since the Alders hadn't been on the trail before, they were a great help in showing Bob where markers were needed. About a mile in, Bob stopped. They were on a hillside that gently descended toward a gully on their left. Beyond the gully was a hill that was lower in elevation than the place where they were standing. Past this hill, some distance to the southeast, they could see the broad valley floor where they lived.

"Is that our house way over there, Ranger Bob?" asked Matty.

"It's over there somewhere, but you'd be hard pressed to see it, even with binoculars," he told her.

Bob put down the trees and grabbed his shovel. He walked up the hill and started digging the first of three holes. Mr. Alder put down the trees he was carrying and went to take turns digging with Bob. The rest of the hiking party took a snack and water break, except for Amos, who was helping widen the holes, wondering if there would be any bones to uncover. Digging the three holes went quickly—the forest soil was loamy and fine here. The men planted the locust, cucumber magnolia, and dogwood about thirty feet apart in a triangular pattern. With the last of the dirt tamped into place, the party resumed hiking up the trail toward a peak about a mile and a half ahead of them. Along the way Bob continued to put up markers, and take soil samples.

Sassafras Knob marked the halfway point of the hike, and from its peak they could see for miles in every direction. The knob was a rocky limestone outcropping jutting up from the ridge line. Only a few crooked pine trees grew on the peak, their roots twisting around the limestone to find toe-holds in the cracks. The hikers rested and ate lunch together. Matty and Ryker looked around with their parents' binoculars and found a red-tailed hawk looking for its lunch as it circled a neighboring peak. The kids followed the hawk's soaring until it ducked out of sight behind a hill. The sight of the graceful bird made Matty and Ryker long to be flying over the mountains again.

After finishing their lunch, the hikers headed north-ward and down from the knob toward another valley. Mountain pines surrounded them as they walked along the trail, their snaky roots often exposed to view. Bob pointed out, a white-breasted nuthatch and Carolina wren flitting in the pines as they walked downward. Another mile of hiking brought them to a section of trail with a gentler descent that paralleled a stream. The water ran toward the small valley below. Thick stands of mountain laurel and mountain fetterbush grew along the stream's banks taking advantage of the moisture it provided. The fetterbush would bloom in a few weeks with bunches of bell-like white flowers dangling toward the ground. In the air the hikers could hear a waterfall announcing itself with loud rumblings. Soon the small falls came into view between the laurels, and the hikers could see its waters sparkling in the midday sunlight. Everyone paused briefly to enjoy the sight and sound of the rushing water, but soon they continued their single file procession to the valley below.

Walking out onto the valley floor, they found the woods opening into a wide green meadow lush with new spring grasses. The trail followed the stream back and forth through the meadow. In the middle of the meadow, Bob stopped everyone again. It was time to plant the remaining trees. With Amos' help, Bob and Mr. Alder dug three more holes and got the trees planted in the ground. Matty, Ryker, and Mrs. Alder spent the time sitting on the stream bank watching a family of ducks swimming against the current. When the work was finished, they followed the trail out of the valley and up another part of the hill they'd descended. Another mile of hiking brought them to the top of the ridge and back to the access road near their starting point. "We made a big loop!" Ryker announced to everyone.

Everyone was tired—the hike had taken about three-and-a-half hours—so Bob suggested they head to another spot just down the road to relax before making the drive home. A good nap sounded like just the thing to Mr. and Mrs. Alder. They coaxed the kids into the truck and drove with Bob up the main road to another access road. The access road ran by a broad field the rangers kept mowed for overnight-campers. Bob drove across the field and parked next to a massive lone oak tree standing in the middle of the grassy area. Here they could lay down in the soft grass and rest. Mrs. Alder took a couple of Ranger Bob's blankets and spread them in the shade offered by the truck and still-bare tree. The adults stretched out and were talking when Ryker asked, "Can we go look around the field and woods?" He didn't feel like napping and neither did Matty. This was a new place and they wanted to explore.

Mr. Alder looked up at Ryker, Matty, and Amos and said, "I don't mind if you go exploring, but don't run far off. We're not staying here *that* long."

Matty and Ryker put on their backpacks and the three friends went to explore the perimeter of the field. They made a wide circle around the adults as they walked along the field's edge. After making one loop, they decided to broaden their exploration and walk through the woods just beyond the edge. On the far side, opposite from where Ranger Bob had driven onto the field, the three friends walked into the forest. As they walked, they found that the ground, which had been flat all around the field, was now starting to descend. Going down a gentle slope, they walked through last year's dead leaves, crunching them with each step. They couldn't see the field above them and decided not to wander down the hill. Instead, they walked parallel to the perimeter again, slowly lengthening their arc. Something in the distance ahead of them caught their attention. The rich brown, gray, and green colors of the woods were disturbed by a number of lightly colored areas. Matty and Ryker both stopped as they tried to distinguish what the bright patches were.

"Matty, what are those white spots over there?" asked Ryker.

"I can't make them out; they're too far away," she said.

Amos, who had been sniffing through some large leaf piles, perked up his ears and sniffed the wind that was blowing from the direction of light colors. They walked on, slowly getting closer. Amos ran ahead and the kids could see him sniffing as he circled the whitish patches, which were two- to three-hundred feet down and away from the perimeter of the field. Matty and Ryker ran to discover what this strange sight was. Ryker was the first to identify the bright spots, and yelled, "They're tree stumps,

Matty." As they both approached, they found they had been looking at a number of freshly cut tree stumps. The exposed wood from the stumps looked white in the bright sun. They also found piles of sawdust scattered around where the trees had been cut into sections.

"Ryker, these trees must have been cut just a few days ago. Look how bright the stumps are."

"I know, Matty. And look how many there are! There must be twenty trees gone. Are you allowed to cut down trees in the National Forest?"

"You can cut firewood somewhere because the guy who brings our firewood gets it from the forest. But remember Ranger Bob tells us that we should never take anything out of the forest—like rocks, bugs, or plants. Maybe we'd better go ask him about these missing trees!"

"Let's investigate a little, then we can give Ranger Bob a full report, just like real rangers," Ryker told Matty.

Matty agreed this would be the wise thing to do. They walked to the stumps one by one and felt the ridges made from the chain saw cutting through the trunk. Sawdust was laying all around and it made Matty think about Ranger Bob's soil samples. She picked up her own samples to show the ranger—two pockets full of sawdust.

Ryker was upset about how many trees were gone. The forest looked pretty bare to him in this spot. *How long would it take to grow new trees here?* he wondered.

"New *trees!*" Ryker yelled to Matty. "I'm brilliant. We can plant some new trees to replace these old ones. You have your stick, don't you Matty?"

"It's here in my backpack. That *is* a brilliant idea. But we need to do it before we go get Ranger Bob, or he'd know they weren't here when he first looked around," she said.

"No problem. Just pull it out and let's get busy before we go to give our report."

Matty pulled the stick and case out of her backpack. She wanted to be very careful not to plant trees where she didn't mean to. *How do I do this?* she thought. Finally she figured out that she needed something to grasp the stick with, like Ryker had done earlier with his hat.

"Your hat, Ryker! I need your hat. Then I can hold the stick and touch it right before I hit the ground. That way we don't get trees growing that we didn't mean to plant."

Ryker took off his hat and gave it to Matty. She gripped the stick with the hat, swung it over her head, and, as she brought it down to the ground, she touched the stick with her thumb. When she finished hitting the ground, she lifted her thumb from against the wood of the stick. The three friends watched as a sapling began to rise. The sight of this was still amazing to see, even though they'd watched it before. They walked around the area planting more trees in the same way, being careful all the time about when they touched the crooked stick.

"Make 'em bigger, too, Matty," said Ryker. "Whack 'em and give 'em a boost." Matty went back around and struck the saplings. She struck them each a few times until they were growing noticeably.

As the friends were planting their tenth tree, Amos turned into the wind, sniffed, and started growling. "What's wrong, buddy? What do you smell?" asked Matty. He continued to growl. He was watching a small outcropping of rocks below, around which there were many mountain laurels growing.

"What is he growling at Matty?" asked Ryker.

All three friends were now looking at the rock formation. Matty and Ryker were getting a little nervous. *What was over there? Was it a bear?* they wondered.

"Ryker, I think we better go tell Ranger Bob about the missing trees," Matty said. She was a little nervous and wanted to get away from whatever was making Amos growl.

"Right. I'm with you." Ryker said. He wanted to get out of there, too.

Amos started barking wildly, making Matty and Ryker really nervous. Next they heard a rustling noise among the mountain laurels. Amos bolted down the hill after the noise.

"Somebody is in the bushes, Matty," Ryker yelled. "Look there's two people. They're running toward the rocks."

Two men had been watching the children and were now hurrying away with Amos on their tails. Amos jumped into the bushes just as the second man was going behind the rock formation. A few seconds later, Matty and Ryker heard one of the men yell in pain and then start cussing at Amos. This was followed by the sound of an engine starting, and then one of the men yelling for the other to "COME ON." Amos had been growling loudly through all of this, but suddenly he let out an enormous yelp of pain.

The kids were feeling sick now. "Where was Amos? Was he injured? What should they do?" They heard the hollow metallic sound of a truck-door slamming closed, and then the roar of the truck engine as it sped away through the woods. They couldn't see any of this; it was all going on behind the rocks

"Ryker, get somebody! Quick! We have to help Amos!" Matty screamed.

He was running even before she finished talking. Ryker didn't have to run far. He was almost cresting the hill at the edge of the field when he ran into the adults. They had heard Amos' yelp and Matty's scream and were running down to find out what the trouble was.

"Ranger Bob! Dad! Come quick. They're hurting Amos!" Ryker said. He turned and ran back toward Matty. The Alders and Ranger Bob ran fast to catch him. They were all panting from adrenaline as they ran up to Matty. She was near the laurel bushes, where she'd moved closer to try to help Amos.

"They're getting away, Ranger Bob!" Matty screamed frantically. "I can't find Amos!" She was pointing to the laurels and rock formation. Ranger Bob grabbed the backpack he was wearing and ran toward the laurels.

Mrs. Alder held the children tightly next to her. Mr. Alder followed Bob and both went through the laurels slowly. They were gone for what seemed like an eternity to Mrs. Alder and the children.

After some time had passed Amos came walking through the bushes. Matty and Ryker let out squeals of joy when they saw him and their mother let them go to greet their friend. She was concerned, however; something just didn't look right about Amos. When he came closer they could see that Mrs. Alder's concerns were justified. Amos was hurt and had blood running down from a cut above his eye. He had lunged into a run as soon as he'd seen Matty and Ryker, and when he got close enough jumped on the children with tongue licking. Mrs. Alder tried to hold him back and put a handkerchief over the cut—he was smearing blood on the children.

Mr. Alder emerged from behind the rocks. He also ran up to the children, grabbed them in a bear hug and squeezed. It was a few minutes more until Ranger Bob finally came through the laurels, and Ryker noticed it right away—Ranger Bob was carrying a gun.

"Where'd you get that gun Ranger Bob?" he asked with a look of awe on his face.

"I pulled it out of my backpack, Ryker. Most of the rangers carry 'em now. There's a lot of bad things happening in the forest these days. You haven't seen my gun before because I haven't been wearing it on my belt—haven't quite gotten used to the idea of having to wear a gun around here. After today that's gonna change, though. Now you both tell me what you saw."

The kids recounted their exploration of the hill investigation of the tree cuttings, and encounter with the two men. Ranger Bob listened attentively, taking in every piece of information. After hearing their report, he spent a few minutes surveying the tree stumps. Finally he said to the Alders, "We've been trying to catch these tree thieves for the better part of a year now. They come to a remote area like this, cut down some choice hardwood trees, and then disappear. This is the closest we've come to seeing them. Did you two get a look at them?"

"No, we couldn't see them, and their truck was behind the rocks," Matty told him.

Ranger Bob said, "That's bad luck for me. I was hoping you'd be able to help me find out who they are. Amos ripped off a piece of somebody's pant leg; but that won't get us very far. It looks like they tried to bust open his head with a stick. How's his eye Karen?

"I don't think he'll need stitches, but he's got a nasty bump."

"No wonder he gave out that yelp," Bob said. He paused for a moment, then blared out, "Boy, I'd like to catch those thieves. They headed down the hill toward another fire road. There's no catching them now. I'm sure they've reached the main road and are long gone. The other rangers are at that meeting, so I can't radio them to help." Bob shook his head in disgust then walked over to survey the tree stumps closely.

The Alders looked after Amos' wound and waited for Bob to finish looking around; but Mrs. Alder finally interrupted him and said, "Bob, if you can't catch the thieves today, and are about finished with your inspection, I think it'd be best to get the children home."

"Yes, Karen, I should get you right home. I'll send the sheriff out here tomorrow to look around. Sorry to keep you waiting so long; it's just that this kind of thing really irks me."

Ranger Bob turned toward the field and started walking up the hill to the truck with the Alders following. Halfway up the hill the children remembered they'd dropped their backpacks when Amos had run after the thieves. They ran back down and picked up the packs, while their parents waited for them. Matty secretly packed her crooked stick away without her parents seeing it. She and Ryker then hurried back up the hill to rejoin their parents. Back at the truck the Alders found Ranger Bob standing with his first aid kit ready to disinfect Amos' wound. After a few minutes of cleaning, Amos was looking almost as good as new.

It was a silent drive home in the ranger's truck. Mr. and Mrs. Alder were thinking how glad they were that their kids hadn't been hurt and that Amos would be fine. Ranger Bob was wondering when and how he would catch the thieves. Matty and Ryker were also thinking about thieves—they seemed to be following them everywhere they went.

SPIES ARE WATCHING

THE FLATBED TRUCK was barreling down the country road with its load of stolen logs concealed under a large tarp. Chop Arborcide sat behind the wheel and watched the mirrors as he drove. His brother Buzz was in the passenger seat next to him. Every few seconds Buzz would hang his head out the window to scan the road behind them. It had been a close call for them, but they were feeling safer and safer as they put distance between themselves and the forest.

Earlier in the day, as Ranger Bob had driven into the overnight-camping field, the Arborcide boys had been covering up their truck full of logs. Now they were making off with that load—their third batch of stolen logs taken from this secluded section of forest, all on the same day. Felling the trees and cutting them into long sections had only taken about an hour, and the mechanical arm on the truck made quick work of the loading. The riskiest part was hauling the logs over public roads back to their farm. There was always a chance someone would notice their covered loads. So Buzz and Chop usually never hauled more than one load from a single spot, and between loads they would lay low for a few weeks. Today, however, they had found so many good lumber trees close together, and the area seemed so secluded that they had gotten greedy and broken all their rules. Everything had gone smoothly with the first two loads and it looked as if they were going to get away with the third. But then, just as they were getting ready to drive away, a ranger showed up.

Driving off was impossible. The noise would have given them away. So, they went up to see who was interrupting their work. Fear struck them both when they saw the red and blue lights on top of the ranger's truck. How could they get away now? They watched as the Alders and Ranger Bob got out of the truck and prepared to nap. This was good luck, they thought. The ranger wasn't there to investigate—he was just loafing with some friends. All Buzz and Chop had to do was wait until they left.

But when those kids starting snooping around, the Arborcide boys realized they weren't going to get off so easily. They were forced to sneak back down the hill. And since their truck was parked behind the rock formation, they made a beeline into the cover of the thick bushes in front of the rocks. They wouldn't be spotted there, they thought, and there they could wait until the children went back to the field. But again, they weren't going to be so lucky.

Once Amos came toward them, they had no alternative except to try to make a run for it. Amos wasn't going to let them get away. He had a sense they were dangerous. Amos clamped down on Buzz's calf as he tried to flee. Buzz grabbed a stick and hit Amos hard. Not hard enough, though. Amos didn't let go. By this time, Chop had the truck engine running and was yelling for Buzz to get a move on. Buzz hit Amos a second time even harder. As the stick crashed into Amos' skull just above the eye, Buzz shook his leg and was able to get free. He dashed for the truck and slammed the door behind him. Amos was a bit dazed, but managed to make one last spring toward the truck door just as Chop floored the accelerator and went tearing down the hill toward the fire road.

Now the Arborcides were a number of miles down the road, away from the Alders and Ranger Bob. The pressure of being caught was easing up inside them. They started to think about what they'd seen.

"Chop, they grew trees like it was nothin'!"

"I know. She was hittin' the ground with that stick and them trees was just poppin' up—like groundhogs in spring," he said to Buzz.

"And did you see her hit 'em again? They shot up some more!" Buzz said in amazement. He paused, then insisted, "We've gotta git that stick. Pa'd want it if he'd seen it."

"You's right, brother. We need to git that stick. But first we gotta find out who them folks is, *then* we can do the stealin'."

"I *know* who they is. That scrawny fella's the one Pa almost hit with the truck. Remember, I told you about him? Daggone fool wouldn't get off the road. Somebody down at Jessie's Diner told me his name's Alder," said Buzz. A wide satisfied grin broke on Buzz's face, because he knew where to find both the stick *and* the dog that had bitten him. His leg was throbbing now, and he was thinking about ways to make Amos hurt. He turned to Chop and said menacingly, "I'm gonna kill that dog."

"So, you know where he lives?" Chop asked.

"Yeh, I seen his house. Looked his address up in the phone book and drove by after he almost wrecked us."

Chop thought for a moment, came up with a plan, and said, "Okay. We need to stash this load of logs first. Then we git home, git the car, and go pay a visit to these Alder folks. Maybe we'll even spy that dog. I think he liked the taste of you, brother." Chop laughed.

"Shut up or I'll shut you up myself. When I get my hands on that dog, he won't be bitin' anything again, believe you me," Buzz snarled. He looked out the passenger's window again. Chop laughed about the dog once more, and then lapsed into thought about the tree stick.

The Arborcide boys took the load of logs to a secret lumber mill they operated on the edge of their farm. At their father's direction, they had been stealing wood from the National Forest, processing the logs in the mill, and selling the finished lumber to a wood dealer in a neighboring state who thought the wood was from a private lot. It was risky business, but the Arborcides had become experts at dodging the rangers and sheriff's deputies. They'd been in operation an entire year without a run-in with the law. They used special scanners to keep track of the rangers' and deputies' movements; and they made friends with them at the diner to get useful bits of information.

The secret mill stood in a thick grove of white pines. The Arborcide boys had strung camouflage netting over the mill building and their wood lot so the lumber operation couldn't be easily detected. Chop and Buzz pulled through the netting into the lot, parked the truck, and made sure it was hidden from view. When they'd gotten everything settled, they rode their four-wheel drive ATVs back to their farmhouse. Mr. Arborcide wasn't around, and his truck was gone. So, Buzz and Chop got the keys to their car from the house, hopped in, and headed off toward town to spy on the Alders.

The Alders and Ranger Bob, meanwhile, had packed up their blankets and headed back to town. It was late afternoon as the truck pulled up to the Alder residence. Everyone was tired from the hike, especially the men, since they had carried and planted the trees. As they unloaded their gear, Mr. and Mrs. Alder were thinking about getting cleaned up and relaxing. Ranger Bob wasn't going to get a chance to rest. He needed to get to work on the tree thefts. He said, "Ben, Karen, I'm real sorry about the scare the kids got today. I'm sure glad Amos wasn't hurt badly." Bob looked at the kids, then bent down and scratched Amos' back. Straightening up he said, "I've got to get over to the sheriff's right away and have them start investigating this new incident. Hopefully we can get to the bottom of it."

"I hope so," said Mrs. Alder. "It's just awful to think about the things people are doing around here these days."

"And it seems like we've been right in the middle of it this week," Mr. Alder added. Everyone was silent for a moment. Mr. Alder said, "We'd better let you go and get to work Bob. Thanks for the hike today. *That* part of the day was beautiful. I love springtime in the valley."

"The forest *was* gorgeous today, I must admit. I'd better get a move on now. You all get rested up. I probably won't see you until church next Sunday; that is, unless we turn something up on these thieves. One more thing. The sheriff might want to talk to you and the kids."

"That's fine. Tell him to call us if he needs to," said Mr. Alder.

Bob acknowledged this with a nod, said good-bye to everyone, and got in his truck. He headed out of the driveway toward town and the sheriff's office. Mr. and Mrs. Alder picked up all the family gear, including Matty's backpack with the stick in it, and went to the mud room door. Matty and Ryker were hanging back in the driveway and Mr. Alder asked, "Hey, aren't you two coming in for a rest?"

"I'm not tired, Dad. I think I'll play outside some more since it's such a nice day," Matty answered.

"Me too, Dad," added Ryker.

"Okay, but stay in the yard." Their dad and mom went into the house to get cleaned up before going to the living room to relax and read a book together. Meanwhile, Ryker and Matty took some time to wrestle with Amos in the front yard. After a few minutes of wrestling, Ryker was on the ground with Amos on top of him. Matty was pulling Amos by the tail trying to get him off. Suddenly Ryker's eyes widened and he said, "Matty, we forgot about the experiment we started this morning." With a surge of energy he shoved Amos off of his chest, got on his feet, and dashed across the driveway behind the garage. Matty and Amos looked at each other and then started after him. When they caught up, Ryker was standing in front of the patio stones near the compost pile. In front of him was a line of small saplings. They were right underneath the line he had traced in the air earlier in the day. The experiment had worked! And it showed that the stick worked without having to touch the ground. Once again, there were no saplings growing on top of the patio stones. The stick couldn't make trees grow unless there was soil in which to grow them.

Matty came up beside Ryker and inspected the saplings. "Ryker, I *knew* the stick must work this way. So, I was the one who made all those trees spring up in Mr. Arbor-cide's field. I wish I'd known about this earlier."

Ryker was listening to her and thinking hard at the same time. He scratched his head and finally said to her. "Matty, these trees aren't that big. How did the ones in Arborcide's field grow so fast? He was ticked because the saplings were big enough to mess up his equipment."

Matty puzzled for a minute and said, "I was really tense while we were banking over the field. I bet it has something to do with how I was feeling! Maybe when you're scared or excited it makes the stick work better."

"I still can't believe you were scared at those little banking maneuvers! *Girls!*" said Ryker sarcastically.

"Well there must be a line of giant trees out on 259, as thrilled as you were with yourself on the Horst's wagon," Matty shot back.

Ryker ignored Matty's dig and said, "Hey, I don't remember Mom saying anything about saplings all along the road; the road crew probably didn't wait long enough to see them growing. Didn't you say they dug up the big ones at night–the ones where we were striking the road."

"Yes! For your information I did say that. At least you're paying attention to something I say."

"Oh calm down, Sis! I was only joking about you being wimpy. Anyway, if the saplings in the road aren't any bigger than these, a car could run them over, no problem. In fact, I bet they've already gotten squashed. We're in the clear there."

Ryker pondered some more, then said, "The Horsts! Matty, they must have seen the bigger trees on their way home the other night. Remember? They had to go back out 259 to get to their house."

"Ryker, do you think it could have been the Horsts who reported the trees to the sheriff?"

"It must have been! They went right back that way going home. Do you think they might suspect *us?*" he asked.

"Ryker, the Horsts didn't see the tree when we were on the wagon. They were looking at me when I screamed. Then I gave them that spider story. If they'd seen the fir tree, they'd have said something right then."

"So, we're in the clear on that one too?

"I think so."

"Okay. We've got a magic stick. What do we do with it?" Ryker asked.

"*Magic!* Ryker, you're brilliant."

"Well, I know that! I'm glad you're finally realizing it."

"Oh, don't let your head get too big and fat to carry. What I mean is that it's *magic*. Do you remember that little rhyme Miss Anne and Miss Sue told us? It said, 'Hold the *wand* with care ye saints. . . . ' Remember?"

"Now that you say it, I remember. But what does it mean?"

"The stick is a *wand*. It's like a magic tree planting wand. *That's* why we're supposed to hold it with care. We can plant trees whenever we're holding it."

"Not anywhere. Remember, it can't grow them in concrete."

"How could *I* forget that? Remember *I'm* the one who showed *you* about it."

"All right. I just didn't want you to forget."

"Ryker, we could plant new trees wherever people need them. Think about it. We could replant the dead places in the National Forest."

"No, I've got something even better. We could go to Brazil or Indonesia and replant the rain forest. *That* would be cool."

"And just how do you suppose you're going to *get* to Brazil or Indonesia?"

Ryker bowed and said in his TV commentator voice, "Ladies and gentlemen, I present Dr. Ryker Daniel Alder, galactically renowned tree expert and keeper of the magic tree wand. We have invited him and his assistant, Ms. Madeline Alder, on an all-expense paid expedition to restore our rain forest."

"Oh brother, your head is swelling. You just remember that I'm not an assistant. I am co-finder and keeper of the wand. Who figured out what it could do? *Me!*"

"All right, all right, we'll go to Brazil as co-keepers of the wand. When do we get started?"

"Ryker, we have to work up to things like that. First we need to start planting trees here. Then we can work up to other places. I suggest we start using the stick whenever we're in the forest. We can even plant some trees around town—in secret."

"I'm agreeable to that, but I want to get to Brazil before I'm twenty."

"Why twenty?"

"'Cause I don't want to go when I'm an old man, like Dad."

Matty laughed at this. Their dad wasn't even forty yet, and he was in great shape. She shook her head and said, "Ryker, let's go in and get cleaned up. We know what to do with the wand now. We're going to have some good adventures. It's like we've received a special work to accomplish. We're the keepers of something magical."

"Yeh, it's too cool. Wait 'til I tell everybody."

"Wait a minute. We need to keep this quiet for a while. We've got to do this in secret."

"Secret? What are you talking about? I want to tell everybody. How are we ever going to get to Brazil if nobody knows about it?"

"Ryker, that just won't do. If we tell people *now*, they'll take the stick away from us. I'm not even 11 and you're only 9. Do you think they'd let us keep the stick?"

"Mom and Dad wouldn't take it away from us."

"It's not *them* I'm worried about. It's other people. You know, like some researcher. We need to wait 'til we get older to tell people."

"You know, I think you're right. My spy books talk about all kinds of stuff government agents can do. They could knock us out with some kind of gas and take the wand. We wouldn't know it until we woke up. Or they could use those silent helicopters to swoop down and surround us when we're in the forest." Matty was rolling her eyes at this point. Ryker continued, "We better keep this under wraps, Agent Matty. Let's refer to it as code name "Crooked Wand." For our eyes only. Roger?"

"Yes 007," she said mockingly, "Mum's the word." Matty was thinking her brother was an over-dramatic weirdo, but if it helped him keep the secret, she was willing to go along with it. "Let's go inside now. It's getting close to dinnertime."

"First, let's get rid of these saplings. We don't want anything laying around for the spies to find. They might be able to see these with satellite surveillance." Ryker started pulling up the small trees and putting them on the compost pile. Matty helped him and was smiling on the inside about all the spy stuff. When they were finished, they headed into the house with Amos to get cleaned up for dinner.

As they walked in the back door, neither of them noticed that a gray car was parked on the shoulder of the road not far from their house.

AMOS GETS GROUND BY
THE GRINDER

MR. AND MRS. ALDER were in the family study when the three friends came in the mud room door. As they walked through the kitchen, the smell of food made them all hungry. Mrs. Alder had some frozen vegetable soup thawing on the stove, and Mr. Alder had whipped together some Irish soda biscuits that were cooking in the oven. Matty and Ryker made their way into the study with Amos. Mr. and Mrs. Alder were sitting on the loveseat taking turns reading a novel aloud to each other. When they saw the kids, they put down the novel and looked up. Mrs. Alder said, "Hello, you three. Have you had enough wrestling for the evening?"

"We're worn out, Mom," Ryker said. "When do we get to eat?"

"Dinner should be ready in another fifteen minutes. You both need to get cleaned up before that, so run on upstairs. Then make sure to feed Amos."

Matty and Ryker made their way upstairs, and Ryker took the first turn in the bathroom. Matty walked into her bedroom and saw her backpack lying on the floor where her mom had placed it. She pulled out the magic wand, still snug inside its case, and felt it for a moment. All the images of the day came flying into her mind: the hike,

Ranger Bob, the meadow and ducks, the tree thieves. Just then, Ryker got out of the shower and yelled, "I'm done." This startled Matty out of her daydream and she quickly put the stick under her bed and took her turn in the bathroom. A bath and fresh clothes felt good to her.

When she joined everyone in the kitchen, Ryker was pouring water in the glasses, while Mr. and Mrs. Alder were bringing the soup and biscuits to the table. Matty filled Amos' bowl with dog food before she sat down. The family prayed and the kids dug into the biscuits. Mrs. Alder ladled soup into bowls and Mr. Alder passed them around. When each of them tasted the soup, they just kept eating without talking for a while. They were famished, and the soup was thick and filling.

Mrs. Alder was the first to speak. She said, "Matty and Ryker, I forgot to tell you that Mrs. Horst called this evening to invite you to visit the dairy farm tomorrow. Miss Anne is going to be visiting too."

"Really, Mom? Boy they sure are nice folks," Ryker said.

Matty was hesitating and asked, "Can we go Mom? I mean, what about you and Dad? You guys took the week off to be with *us*. Seems like we'd be dumping you. What will you do?"

Mr. Alder smiled and said, "That is very considerate of you, Matty. I think we can get by for a few hours tomorrow. What do you think Karen?"

"Oh, I suppose we can. Are you sure you two want to visit the farm?"

"Are you kidding, Mom?" said Ryker. "I bet they have some great equipment to ride on. Y' know, Mennonite folks *do* have tractors and stuff. They just don't have cars."

"Yes, I think we knew that, son," said Mr. Alder. "And I bet you just might finagle a tractor ride out of Mr. Horst."

"Cool!" Ryker exclaimed.

"Did you tell her we were coming, Mom, or do we need to call?" Matty asked.

"You need to call to confirm things with Mrs. Horst . . . *after* you get the dishes cleaned up," said Mrs. Alder.

"I'm finished with my dinner," Matty said. "Can I get started cleaning up?"

"Yes, go right ahead," her mom told her.

Matty took her plate to the sink and rinsed it off. Ryker followed with his bowl and Mr. Alder's. Mr. and Mrs. Alder talked while the kids cleaned off the rest of the dishes and put them in the dishwasher. The family had a rule about meals: whoever cooks doesn't have to clean up. So, often the kids did the dishes. But not always. Sometimes they cooked meals like: fettuccini alfredo, pesto pizza, and veggie burgers.

After the kitchen was clean, Matty let Amos outside, then went to the phone and called Mrs. Horst. They arranged to visit tomorrow after lunch—this would give the kids time to see the farm before the evening milking. Mrs. Horst told Matty that Amos was invited too.

With that settled, Matty let Amos back in and the Alders went into the study to spend the evening reading and playing cribbage together. When they finally turned in, it didn't take long for everyone to go to sleep. Even Amos, whose cut over his eye was still smarting, crashed next to Matty's bed—under which lay the magic wand.

On Monday, Mrs. Horst had talked to Miss Anne about having met her friends the day before and that she wanted the children to visit the farm. Miss Anne decided right away that, since she was coming over to visit the Horsts on Wednesday afternoon, it would be the perfect time for the children to visit. It was spring break, and Miss Anne knew Mr. and Mrs. Alder would enjoy some time alone during the kids' week off. Mrs. Horst agreed this was a good time for the kids to visit and called Mrs. Alder to invite them.

Wednesday morning at the Alders' was spent cleaning the house and working in the sunroom. Everyone pitched in to get the regular cleaning done. Then, while the children and Mr. Alder went into the sunroom to work, Mrs. Alder dug into a few spring cleaning projects she wanted to accomplish. Much needed to be done to get ready for garden planting. Mr. Alder had asked his friend, Tom Smallet, to come plow the garden area with his tractor. So when he arrived, Ryker and Matty got to take a break from working to watch the tilling with their dad and Amos. Tom Smallet had an old red Massey-Ferguson tractor with a shiny new orange rototilling implement on the back. He churned up the garden soil in about fifteen minutes with his tiller. Matty and Ryker ran through the soft dirt, picking up handfuls of it to test the consistency. They determined it was ready for planting. After the excitement of plowing was over, they went back inside to finish their work in the sunroom.

At noontime, as they sat down for grilled tuna fish sandwiches with chips, everyone was feeling as if they'd accomplished something good. There was to be no lingering over lunch, however, because the kids wanted to get to the Horst's soon. Matty and Ryker ate hurriedly and kept staring at their dad, who was eating slowly. When they finished their sandwiches, Mr. Alder told them to go get their things together and he would be ready when they returned. The three friends ran upstairs, and the kids got their jackets and backpacks together. Matty reached under the bed and got the tree wand which she had decided to take with her. When she and Ryker got back to the kitchen, Mr. Alder was standing in front of the sink just finishing his sandwich. Mrs. Alder kissed Matty and Ryker good-bye as they headed out to the garage. "Be sure to call if you need anything. We'll be here," she said.

"We will, Mom. Love you," Matty told her.

They put on their boots in the mud room and then went outside. Mr. Alder followed them out and called to Mrs. Alder, "I'll be back in a few minutes, Honey. Do you need me to pick up anything while I'm out?"

"No. I just need *you*, this afternoon," Mrs. Alder said smiling.

They jumped into the car and drove off toward the Horsts. A gray sedan parked on a side road near their house turned onto the road behind them. Mr. Alder noticed the car, but didn't give it a second thought.

They arrived at the Horst farm within minutes. Matty and Ryker thought about how much shorter the ride was by car than by buggy, and how long it would have taken them to walk home Sunday afternoon. As they turned into the long gravel driveway, they saw Mrs. Horst and Miss Anne sitting on the porch of the farmhouse. The ladies saw them as well and came down from the porch to meet them. Mr. Alder parked the car next to the house. The kids and Amos jumped out to greet the ladies. Amos found a bush to mark first thing. Matty apologized, but Mrs. Horst said, "That's what dogs do. It's their way of greeting." Standing with the car door open and one foot still inside Mr. Alder told the ladies he'd come back about 5 P.M.—sooner if they needed. The kids got their backpacks and jackets out of the car and told their dad good-bye. He was about halfway up the drive when Miss Anne said to the three friends, "Well, what a nice surprise to see you twice in one week."

"It sure is. And we're glad you know the Horsts," Matty replied. "They really saved us the other day."

"So I hear."

"We can't thank you and Mr. Horst enough," Ryker said. He looked around and asked, "Where is Mr. Horst? Is he out on a tractor?"

"No, Ryker. He's looking over some of the cows. Would you two like to take a look at our herd?"

"Boy, would we ever!" he yelled.

They walked down a path behind the house to the large barn and milking house. Two very tall dark-blue silos stood at one end of the barn, along with a shorter one that was dull gray. Mrs. Horst pointed to them and said, "That's where we keep the silage for our cows. The corn gets chopped up at harvest time and put in there. Conveyor belts move it into the barn where the cows eat it."

To the left of the silos was the door into the milking house. They went around to the door. Matty stopped before following Mrs. Horst in and asked, "Is it okay if Amos comes inside?"

"Yes, that's fine, Matty. He's going to get a little dirty, though. So, you'll probably need to hose him down before you go home."

"Oh, that's all right. He gets dirty a lot at home," Matty told her.

Amos walked into the building following Matty. No cows were in the milking house. The Horsts milked twice a day—in the morning and evening. Mrs. Horst led them through a storage room, which had cabinets and a few stainless steel sinks in it, into the milking room. As Matty and Ryker walked through the doorway, they saw that they were entering something like a pit, which was much longer than it was wide. It seemed like a pit because on three sides of it there was a wide raised walkway with steel railings around the edges so people and cows couldn't fall off. On the two longer sides of the platform there were stanchions constructed from steel pipe for the cows. These stalls were set at an angle to the wall so cows could be maneuvered into them easily.

"At milking time," Mrs. Horst explained, "Mr. Horst or I lead the cows around the platform and back them into the stalls. After we shut them in, whoever is working down here washes up the cows' udders and hooks them to these automatic milking machines." She showed Matty and Ryker a set of four hoses with special ends that attached to a cow's udders. "Once they're hooked up, the milking machine pumps out their milk and sends it to a storage tank in another room. Every other day a man from the dairy plant collects it."

"I get it now. With the cows locked up on the platform, down here you're at eye level with their *privates*," Ryker said.

Mrs. Horst smiled and said, "Yes, that's it exactly."

The room was fascinating to Matty and Ryker. They hadn't seen a big milking operation before. Their grandmother milked her single cow by hand.

Matty asked, "How much milk can you get from a cow?"

"About 70 pounds a day," Mrs. Horst answered.

"You mean gallons?" Ryker asked her.

"No. We measure it in pounds. That way we can know how much butter fat is in it. The milk you drink has had the cream and butter churned out of it," Mrs. Horst told him.

"I never knew so much went into getting milk," Matty said, looking around her.

"There *is* a lot to it. More than most people think about when they pour it out of the plastic jug," said Mrs. Horst. "How about if we go find Mr. Horst now? I think he's in the barn with the cows."

They walked up some steps onto the milking platform and through a door out into the barn. The barn was a large rectangular building with a dirt floor covered with sawdust, straw, and cow manure. In the center of the building was the feeding area. The cows were all standing side by side with their heads locked between metal holders. They had their heads down eating silage from the trough in front of them. *There must be twenty-five cows on either side of the trough*, Matty thought.

Mr. Horst was walking along behind the cows inspecting them with the veterinarian. Ryker ran up to the two men and said, "Hi, Mr. Horst. Why are all the cows lined up?"

"Well hello, Ryker, it's good to see you. The cows are lined up because they're locked in their feeding slots. Dr. Dingledine and I are checking them over. He's a large animal veterinarian." Dr. Dingledine nodded with a smile at Ryker and the others. "We want to make sure the cows are healthy, and also find out where they are in the calving process. That way we can help them have little ones."

"They have babies, Mr. Horst?" Matty asked.

"Oh yes, they have a calf about every year. It keeps their milk coming strong."

"Wow," Matty said looking at all the cows. "A baby every year? What do you do with all those babies?"

"It *is* a lot of calves. We've got about a hundred cows, so we keep Dr. Dingledine pretty busy. Some of the little ones replenish the herd when an older cow dies; others I sell to farmers at the livestock auction."

Mrs. Horst interrupted the conversation saying, "Children, Mr. Horst and Dr. Dingledine need to finish their work. Would you like to watch them for a few minutes? You can see what Dr. Dingledine does with the cows."

Matty and Ryker thought this would be great, and stepped back from the cows as Dr. Dingledine and Mr. Horst continued their work. The kids followed all the activity intently. Dr. Dingledine would check the cows to see if they were pregnant.

The kids had never seen anything like this before and watched for a long time as the men went down one row of cows and then part way up another. After a while, Mrs. Horst asked, "Would you like to go outside and look at the horses and sheep now?"

"Sure," Matty and Ryker said together.

She led them out of the far end of the barn through a large doorway. The sun was shining brightly as they walked into the muddy paddock area where the cows usually stayed when it wasn't milking time. Matty looked down at her feet. Mud and cow manure was caked on them. She was glad she'd decided to wear her boots.

Mrs. Horst asked everyone to wait a moment while she went into a tack room next to the barn. She came out with a feed bag full of oats, and then led the kids over a small hill to a field where the horses were grazing. Dunlap, the horse that had been pulling the Horst's buggy, was running around chasing three younger horses. But not for long. When he saw people standing at the fence line, he galloped over with the other horses following him. Mr. Horst had trained the horses to come to the gate by giving them sweet molasses-coated oats. This way he didn't have to chase them around the field when he needed one of them.

As the horses came up to the fence, Mrs. Horst showed Matty and Ryker how they could feed oats to the horses in the palm of their hand. Matty and Ryker took some oats, held their hands out almost flat, and let the horses pick up the oats with their tongues and lips. Matty got a tingly sensation down her spine as a horse licked her hand—it was Dunlap. She stroked his nose gently as he ate. It felt fuzzy-smooth, damp and warm. When all the oats were gone, they walked over to another field in which a few sheep were grazing. Mrs. Horst picked up a young lamb for the children to touch. Amos was very interested in the lamb, sniffing it all over and nuzzling his nose into its wool. Matty and Ryker each took a turn holding the lamb. This, too, gave Matty that tingly sensation.

Mrs. Horst was putting the lamb down next to its mother when they all heard Mr. Horst motoring up the path pulling a wagon full of hay behind a small tractor.

He slowed down as he neared them and yelled, "Dr. Dingledine and I are finished checking the cows. I thought you all might enjoy a ride around the property. Would you like that?"

"What fun!" Matty said, looking at Mrs. Horst.

"You bet!" Ryker yelled. "Can I ride up there with you?"

"That'd be fine with me. Hop up here on the fender." Ryker climbed up next to Mr. Horst. He had seen Mennonite kids riding next to their fathers like this. Now *he* was getting to do it.

"How about you Matty? Where would you like to ride?" asked Mrs. Horst.

"I think the wagon looks like fun," she said. "Are you and Miss Anne coming?"

"I wouldn't miss a good hayride," said Miss Anne.

The women got onto the hay wagon, and Amos jumped on after them. Mr. Horst turned the tractor back down the hill toward the barn and drove around the manure containment pond.

"What's that concrete thing? It looks like a swimming pool filled with mud," Ryker asked Mr. Horst.

"That's where we wash the manure out of the barn. We keep it in that pool area and then use it to fertilize the fields."

"Whewey! Now I smell it. I sure would hate to fall in there."

"That's why we have the fence around it. Don't want *anything* falling into *that*."

They headed around the barn and down another path that led to some large fields. Rye grass covered the fields that gently sloped southward toward some wooded hills. Beyond these hills were the larger ridges of the National Forest. Ryker was looking around at all the green grass. In the distance to the west he saw some large silos and asked Mr. Horst if these were his also.

"No, Ryker, those are my neighbor's. Our property stops just over there at the gully. Mr. Arborcide owns everything from the gully on over to the hills in the west. Can you see the fence next to the gully?"

Ryker wasn't listening to what Mr. Horst had asked him. He was thinking about Mr. Arborcide. The field way over there was the one they had been flying over and in which they had made trees grow.

"Ryker? Did you hear what I said?" asked Mr. Horst, wondering why Ryker looked dazed.

"I'm sorry. I *did* hear you, but I remembered that we met Mr. Arborcide at the Showalter's the other day. He was plain mean to us."

"Well he can be a difficult man," Mr. Horst replied, not wanting to speak ill of his neighbor.

Ryker continued to look dazed. Mr. Horst wondered about Ryker's encounter with Arborcide as he kept driving down the path toward the forest.

Mrs. Horst had been talking with Matty and Miss Anne about the property. Matty had asked her, "Are all of those woods out there yours? They look like a fun place to go exploring."

"That's right, Amelia. I forgot to tell you the children are natural explorers. Isn't that right Matty?" said Miss Anne.

"Well, Ryker, Amos, and I do like to explore." Amos barked when he heard his name. As they drove, he continued to run around the wagon looking over the sides at the ground below.

Mrs. Horst answered Matty's question. "The woods straight ahead are ours—at least until the National Forest starts on the other side of the hill. See the mountains beyond?" She paused, and Matty nodded her head. "Now over that way," she turned and pointed, "see how the hills curve around and head north? Well, everything past the gully line and around the curve of the hills way over there is Mr. Arborcide's. His property is in between us and the National Forest to the west." She pointed over to the west and north.

"Mr. Arborcide?" Matty asked, feeling scared.

"Why, yes, child. What's wrong?" Mrs. Horst couldn't help noticing that Matty was frightened.

"We met him the other day. He's a mean man. He said some bad things about my dad." Matty was getting all worked up. She took her backpack off and pulled out the magic wand case. She remembered having held it while flying over Mr. Arborcide's field, so she made sure not to touch it. But the stick made her feel at ease for some reason. Ryker was feeling dazed at the same time as Matty.

He finally looked back at her and saw her holding the wand. It made him feel better too, even if he wasn't holding it. Matty was dangling her feet off the rear of the wagon and holding the stick in its case between her legs. If she bent over, she could almost touch the ground with it. The tractor was near the woods now and Mr. Horst was getting ready to turn back toward the house.

The Arborcide boys had followed the Alders to the Horst's home and had seen the kids get out. *What luck*, they thought. Those little brats were right next door to their own farm. Maybe they could get their hands on that stick somehow. They drove on to their farmhouse and got into their camouflage hunting gear. Chop told Buzz to head up into the hills on the four-wheel drive ATV to get a good look at what was going on at the Horst farm. If he saw a chance to steal the stick, then he could radio him about how to sneak over and get it. Buzz got a move on and picked up a pair of binoculars, a spotting scope, and a two-way radio so he could stay in contact with Chop.

First thing, Buzz went by the secret mill on the far side of the hills behind their farm. He wanted to get Grinder. "The Grinder" (as they sometimes called him) was the watchdog the Arborcide boys kept at the mill to make sure nobody came snooping around it. Buzz had trained him to patrol the property, so that if anybody got too close to the white pine grove, he could scare them off. The only people who had ever run into him had been a couple of lost hikers, and they'd high-tailed it away *pronto*.

With The Grinder following him, Buzz hiked over to the hills behind the Horst's property to get a good view of their farm. In the spotting scope, the first thing he saw was the children playing with the lambs. He radioed back that it didn't look like Chop would get a chance to get the stick for a while.

As Buzz continued to watch, the people below got on the tractor. The tractor slowly headed his way and after a long while, turned back toward the barn. It was then that he saw Matty was holding something between her legs. He zoomed the spotting scope in and saw that it was the long case from which he'd seen her take the stick in the forest. It was so close. How could he get his hands on it? Looking down at Grinder, he had an idea. Grinder could get the stick! He'd trained the dog to retrieve things. And nobody knew he was their dog. They'd think he was a wild stray.

Buzz rolled up his backpack to simulate the shape of Matty's case and showed it to the dog. He pointed down at the tractor and said "Retrieve." Grinder knew what to do in an instant. Not only was he mean, he was smart too. He tore off down the hill through the underbrush after the wagon. Buzz slowly backed up to the crest of the hill to make sure he wouldn't be spotted.

Grinder's eyes were fierce with the chase. He wasn't quite sure what he was retrieving at first—the wagon was too far away to make it out clearly. But he knew it was something like the wadded up backpack his master had shown him. Once he saw the case, and understood that that was what he had to retrieve, he didn't take his eyes off it for a second. He had a long way to go to catch up with the wagon, and he was running full speed. Amos was the first to notice him. Grinder was now about three hundred feet behind and gaining quickly. Amos started growling wildly.

Matty said cheerily, "Look, there's a dog chasing us. Is that your dog?"

"No, we don't have a dog right now. But he sure is a big one . . . and look how fast he's running after us," Mrs. Horst said.

Matty was smiling at the dog. She loved animals and always thought the best of them. She wasn't thinking this could be a mean dog and waved her hand at it saying, "Come on, boy. Come on."

Amos began to bark. He had an instinctive understanding of people and other animals, and his sense told him this dog was as mean as a snake. Matty told Amos to settle down and continued to call the dog, "Come on, boy. You sure can run. Come on." Grinder was about a hundred-feet away.

"Matty, now you be careful. You don't know anything about that dog," Miss Anne said.

Ryker and Mr. Horst finally heard Amos' barks, which had gotten louder, over the roar of the tractor engine. They turned around to see what was going on and saw the dog closing on the wagon. Amos had had enough of this. Matty was still calling the dog, motioning it with one hand to come. In the other hand she held the stick between her legs, which were dangling off the back of the wagon. Amos leapt off the wagon and into the path of The Grinder.

The tractor had been moving at a pretty good clip, so Amos' forward momentum toward his enemy was slowed down significantly as he hit the ground only a few yards in front of Grinder. Grinder, meanwhile, had a full head of steam and his one-hundred plus pounds hit Amos like a loaded dump truck. Amos, with teeth bared, managed to get a chunk of fur from The Grinder's side before he was knocked flying. Grinder was undeterred and bounded on toward Matty.

Matty watched as Amos got pounced, and she realized that the dog was vicious. As it rushed towards her with enraged eyes and sharp teeth showing, her legs were flailing as she frantically attempted to get up into the wagon. Miss Anne saw this and grabbed Matty's shirt, trying to pull her back. But Grinder was too fast for both of them. As Matty flailed backward, he made a long last lunge.

Ryker yelled, "*Look out!*"

Mr. Horst was watching and tried unsuccessfully to throw the dog off by revving-up the tractor and swerving. Nevertheless, Grinder was able to grab the case in his mouth and with a writhing twist, he wrenched it from Matty's grasp. Matty fell backward hard as the case broke loose from her hands, and hit her head on the wagon floor. She lifted her throbbing head and with stars in her eyes saw Grinder headed for the hills with her stick.

Mr. Horst stopped the tractor quickly. Everyone was trying to get to Matty to help her, because they didn't know if she'd been bitten.

Meanwhile, The Grinder had a mouth full and was running hard when he saw Amos, who was on his feet again. Amos was limping a bit, but ready to fight—and he wasn't going to meet this dog again without a little speed behind him. He ran as fast as he could and plowed into The Grinder hard and low. This sent the big dog sprawling, but he quickly dropped the case and jumped in for a fight.

Things were intense for a few seconds: dirt flying, teeth chomping with yelps and growls roaring. Grinder was a huge dog and Amos was still reeling from the first hit. He made a crucial mistake and lowered his head at the wrong instant. Grinder latched on unmercifully to the back of his neck, shook it wildly, and ripped the skin open. He kept shaking until Amos was almost senseless. With his opponent dazed, Grinder got back to his retrieving. One last shake sent Amos to the ground. Grinder snapped up the case and flew up the road.

The fight hadn't lasted long enough for anyone to be able to help Amos. Mr. Horst had grabbed a steel bar that he used for repairing fences out of the wagon, and had gotten almost to the fight when Grinder threw Amos down. He was just a second too late to help Amos.

Amos didn't want any help, though, and he wasn't down long. This dog had attacked Matty, taken the stick, and bested him twice. Amos was mad as a hornet and the pain from the cut on his neck only made him want to fight more.

Mr. Horst approached him as he was getting up. He saw a fury in Amos' eyes and knew he shouldn't try to touch him yet. It didn't matter though because Amos didn't give him time to touch him. Bleeding from the neck and unable to run at full speed, he looked at Mr. Horst and ran after Grinder, determined to recover the stick.

DARKNESS DESCENDS

GRINDER RAN BACK toward his master, who was observing everything from the top of the Horst's hill. "*That's* my dog," Buzz said out loud when Grinder smashed into Amos. Elation flooded his body as he watched Grinder get the stick and then tear into Amos for the second time. Buzz had trained Grinder to be mean by entering him in illegal dog fights around the state. Grinder had learned early on that if he wanted to survive, he had to be tougher than any other dog he met, and he had learned his lesson well.

Running into the woods at the edge of the field, Grinder was thinking only about the praise his master would soon give him. Buzz saw Grinder enter the woods and Amos at a distance struggling to follow. He said under his breath, "You want some more, you mangy mutt? Well keep coming; ole Grinder and I'll give it to ya."

Grinder bounded up the hill to Buzz. There wasn't any praise coming for him yet, however, because Buzz was thinking about getting back at the dog that had bitten him. "Come on, boy. Let's git back to the mill and when that mutt catches up to us we'll do him good. That's for certain!"

Struggling up the hill, Amos felt the pain in his neck and right hindquarter. But the pain didn't deter him. He kept following Grinder, stopping often to check the trail. At the top of the ridge, he found a new scent—one he'd smelled before. It was the bad smell of the man he'd bitten yesterday . . . the one who'd hit him with the stick. This made Amos furious. These two somehow knew each other. He didn't know why they were together, but now he was determined to catch them both. He continued tracking them.

Buzz and Grinder made it back to the mill with no sign of Amos behind them. He was coming though. Buzz was sure of it. He went to the flatbed truck, took a big wooden club out of the gun rack, and put the magic wand case in its place. *I'm goin' to ambush this dog, once and for all,* Buzz thought. He took Grinder past the camouflage netting and into the white pines to find a good place to set a trap for Amos. Once they were well hidden, he radioed Chop, "I've got the stick. And I'll have another present for you shortly, so git yerself over here quick." As he listened to Buzz's voice, Chop wondered what this other present was. He jumped onto his ATV and headed to the mill.

Amos, in the meantime, was following the scents slowly and cautiously, stopping frequently to make sure the man and dog hadn't split up. The smells led Amos to the isolated stand of pines. It had been a long trip for him, hurting as much as he was. He made a slow and cautious approach. These two were dangerous, and he needed to get the jump on them.

As Amos walked softly up to the edge of the stand, he couldn't see his opponents, but he knew they were in the pines somewhere. The trees were quite close together with pine branches so thick you couldn't see past them. Amos sniffed the wind and crept quietly around the edge of the pines. He couldn't see or smell the man and dog, but his back was tingling as it sometimes did when danger was close by.

Buzz and Grinder were crouched behind two large pine trees when Amos had approached. Luckily for them, they were down wind of Amos and he couldn't smell them. They watched his slow advance, and became annoyed when he failed to come into the trees where they were waiting. Instead, Amos circled the pine stand and out of sight.

Where has he gone? Buzz wondered. He was irritated, but all he could do was listen and wait.

Amos walked along the edge of the pine trees, sniffing the air. On the far side he picked up the faint scent of his quarry. They were in there somewhere. He crept back the way he had come without making a sound, putting all his stealth tactics to use. As he snuck back toward where he'd first approached the pines, he spotted something. There was just the faintest patch of color that didn't match. It was the dog he'd been hunting. Amos was betting the man wasn't far away. He backed up, picked a line of attack through the trees that would bring him in behind them, and made his charge.

Grinder and Buzz had kept silent watch, not knowing where Amos had gone. When they finally saw Amos, it was too late; *they* were the ones being surprised. On the way in, Amos caught sight of the big man, but decided to try to disable the dog before taking him on. The direction from which he charged was perfect for surprising Grinder. Amos jumped on the big dog's right hindquarter and bit hard. He saw the man coming at him with a stick and wasted no time going after him. Amos dodged a swing of the stick and latched onto the leg he'd bitten once before. He used all his strength to try to bring the man down.

The attack wasn't in Amos' favor for long. Grinder got his senses back quickly and turned to help his master. This meant Amos was faced with a swinging club on one side and biting jaws on another the other. As Amos turned to ward off a bite by Grinder, Buzz made a quick move with the club, knocking him unconscious.

When the tractor had come to a stop earlier, Ryker had jumped down to make sure his sister wasn't hurt. He went to the rear of the wagon with his back to the fleeing dog. From where she was sitting, Matty saw Amos being throttled by the bigger dog. She let out a big scream as Amos fell to the ground, and Ryker turned to see what was going on. Mr. Horst was already next to Amos and about to help him when he ran off after Grinder. Ryker turned and ran after Amos, yelling *"Stop! Amos, stop!"* Mr. Horst caught Ryker as he ran past and said, "Whoa, son. You can't go chasing after those dogs. They've been fighting and got their blood up. I don't want you getting hurt. Never seen that other dog before. He might be wild." They both yelled for Amos to come back, but with no success. Amos was entering the woods, intent on getting back the wand.

Mr. Horst, still holding Ryker's arm, looked down and said, "We need to look after the ladies, then we'll worry about Amos." They walked back to the wagon and found that Matty had hit her head badly, was frightened and shaking uncontrollably. Mr. Horst suggested that they return to the farm house and contact the Alders. He wanted to get the children safely back to the house, in case the crazed dog decided to return.

Ryker objected to going back to the house. He insisted, "What about Amos? He's running after that dog . . . and he's hurt."

"I know, son," Mr. Horst said. "But we need to take care of your sister first, and call your folks. Hopefully, Amos will turn around and come back."

Matty started to cry and said, "I'm worried about Amos, too. Where's he going? We just *can't* leave him."

"Now, now, child. We'll find him," Miss Anne told her. "First let's get you back to the house and contact your parents, then Mr. Horst will go look for Amos."

"I don't *want* to go to the house," Ryker said vehemently.

Miss Anne said calmly but firmly, "Ryker, this is something you need to do. I know it doesn't feel right to leave Amos right now; but we have to think of Matty and everyone's safety. She's scared and has had a nasty bump. Plus that's a violent animal we're dealing with, so you jump up on the wagon. Mr. Horst and your father can look after Amos in a few minutes."

Ryker reluctantly climbed onto the wagon and Mr. Horst fired up the tractor. When they got back to the house, the ladies took the children into the parlor and Miss Anne called their parents. She hung up the phone and said, "Your parents are coming right over." Mr. Horst heard this and walked to the door. He said that while the ladies waited, he'd go and start looking for Amos. Ryker ran to follow him saying, "I'm going with you." He was really worried about Amos.

"Ryker," Miss Anne said. "I think it would be better if you wait until your dad gets here. Then the two of you can help Mr. Horst. Your dad will need somebody to show him where to look." This made sense to Ryker. When his dad got there, they would have three people looking for Amos.

Mr. Horst went outside, unhooked the wagon from the tractor, and drove back to the edge of the woods where Amos had disappeared. He went up the hill in the direction he thought the dogs had headed.

Meanwhile, as the Alders drove to the Horst's farm they were thinking about all the bad things that were happening. "Where is all this coming from?" Mrs. Alder asked her husband.

"I don't know, Karen, but Anne said the kids are not hurt. And we'll find Amos soon enough."

When the Alders drove up to the house, they saw Ryker waiting on the porch for them. As they stepped out of the car, he said, "Matty's inside, Mom. Come on, Dad, we've got to help Mr. Horst search for Amos."

"Just hold on a minute, Ryker," Mr. Alder said. We need to go in and see Matty before I go off searching for Amos."

"But Amos is hurt, Dad," Ryker said emphatically.

"I know, Son, but Matty is our first concern. I love Amos too, but I need to see your sister first."

Mr. and Mrs. Alder went into the house. Ryker paced back and forth across the porch looking in the front door each time he passed to see when his dad would finish. Mrs. Horst had brought some milk and cookies into the parlor for Matty to eat. She thought this might cheer her up a bit. It did—but only a little. When her parents came in, Matty jumped up from the couch and ran to them. Mrs. Alder caught her in her arms. Matty started crying and couldn't stop the tears. Between sobs, she stuttered out, "That dog . . . I thought he was going to bite me . . . he . . . he hurt Amos and . . . and took my wand," she said sobbing.

"Oh, Matty, dear one. You're okay now. We're here," her mother said, trying to comfort her.

"I know, Mom . . . but Amos . . . he's . . . he's hurt and gone," she continued.

"We'll find him, Honey," Mr. Alder assured her. "Ryker and I will go right now and help Mr. Horst look for him. I bet he's not far. You stay here with your mom and the ladies." Mr. Alder started out and Ryker thought, *Finally . . . we're* doing *something!*

They ran past the barn and down the tractor path into the field. It was a long way to the woods, but Mr. Alder was a good runner and Ryker was full of adrenaline. They found the tractor parked at the end of the field and called to Mr. Horst. He was at the top of the ridge and yelled for them to come up. Mr. Horst had been looking all around the far side of the hill as far as his property extended. When they rendezvoused with Mr. Horst, Mr. Alder asked, "Any sign of Amos?"

"I'm afraid not. I've seen some brush and leaves disturbed on the ground heading to the southwest, but no sign of your dog. There were some drops of blood along that trail. The other dog tore Amos' neck up pretty badly, I'm afraid."

"Let's follow Amos' trail then," said Ryker.

"Well, we can't. You see it goes off my property and toward Mr. Arborcide's. He doesn't look kindly on folks traipsing around his place . . . even his neighbors. He's told me that in no uncertain terms. We'll need to go tell him what's going on first," Mr. Horst said.

"But it's an emergency! We've just gotta follow Amos," Ryker said.

"Ryker, you can't trespass on somebody's land. It's against the law. We'll have to ask permission first," Mr. Alder told him.

"Fat chance *he's* gonna give us permission. He's just a nasty old man," Ryker said getting angry.

"Maybe so, Ryker, but we still have to ask. If we went after Amos, it'd be like someone running through our garden or sunroom without asking," Mr. Alder said. Ryker wasn't buying this example. He wouldn't mind people running through the garden to look for their dog. He knew they weren't going to look for Amos now, and all he could do was sulk and worry. He was so angry at Mr. Arborcide.

Mr. Horst saw how hard this was for Ryker. He knew his neighbor was a difficult man, and Ryker had hinted at something that had happened this week. He said to Mr. Alder, "I understand you all had a little run-in with Mr. Arborcide."

"Well we've had a couple of run-ins with him. If it's all the same, I think you probably better go alone to ask permission to search. We don't seem to be his favorite people."

"That'll be fine. I can't say he's partial to me or Mrs. Horst either, but we'll go tell him what's going on and hope he's decent about it."

They walked back to the tractor and rode down to the farmhouse with Mr. Alder and Ryker sitting on the fenders. Back at the house Mr. Alder and Ryker got off. Mr. Horst drove on in the direction of the Arborcide farm. The sound of the tractor alerted the ladies to the men's return and they came out to see if Amos had been found. Mr. Alder filled them in on what they'd seen and what Mr. Horst was doing. *More waiting*, Ryker thought.

To reach the driveway into the Arborcide farm Mr. Horst drove west about a mile to a "T" intersection in the road.

The road to the right led to Ranger Bob's station. Matty and Ryker had come that way on Sunday after their bikes had been stolen. The road to the left went to the Arborcide farm. Mr. Horst turned the tractor in that direction and headed down the gravel road. This was a state road even though the Arborcides owned the land on both sides. As he drove, Mr. Horst passed by two rugged dirt roads on his right that the Forest Service maintained. These were fire access roads that led through the Arborcide farm to the National Forest. Not far past the second access road, Mr. Horst came to the Arborcides' lane. At the end of the lane stood a farmhouse, some sheds, and a barn.

Mr. Horst noticed that Mr. Arborcide's truck was parked under the pole shed next to the house. He brought the tractor to a stop out front and went up to the door to knock. Before he got a chance to knock, however, old man Arborcide yanked open the door and said, "What do you want here?"

Mr. Horst was a gentle man by nature and rudeness didn't sit well with him. He thought it was everyone's duty to live peaceably with their neighbors. Mr. Arborcide never seemed to want to live peaceably with anyone. He thought to himself, *You need to be calm, and try to be kind to this man.* Then he said, "Good day, Mr. Arborcide. Sorry to bother you, but we've had some trouble over at our place with a feral dog."

"What concern is that of mine?" Arborcide snapped.

Mr. Horst again had to think hard about responding kindly to this man. He paused, controlled his emotions, and said, "Mr. Arborcide, this crazed dog came down out of the woods behind my fields and attacked a young girl and her dog that were visiting us. The girl's dog chased that wild animal into the woods. We tried to find him, but he's crossed from my woods into yours heading west toward the forest. And I think he's been hurt."

"I don't care about no dogs, nor about what goes on at yer property, Horst," the old man growled.

"That's fine, Mr. Arborcide, but this animal's hurt and I need permission to search for him in your woods. I won't be long. Right now time is critical. We don't know how badly he's been injured," Mr. Horst said with some impatience.

Mr. Arborcide heard the impatience in Mr. Horst's voice and he got downright ugly with him. The old man liked being ugly, got some kind of pleasure from it. He said, "You just keep yerself off my property, Horst. We don't allow nobody roamin' around through our woods. I don't care if you think the sky's fallin'. No tellin' what you or anyone else would do on my land. So keep yerself off it. I'll tell the boys to have a look around. An' if they find a dog, I'm sendin' 'im to the pound, you can be sure of that. You ought to know better than to let yer animals run onto another man's land. Aren't you a *Mennonite?*" Mr. Arborcide asked this last question deliberately to taunt Mr. Horst. He didn't like "religious people," as he called them.

Some mean thoughts went through Mr. Horst's mind as he listened to Mr. Arborcide. *What's wrong with this man?* he thought. He struggled for a moment to put these bad thoughts out of his head. He wasn't going to return evil for evil; the Scriptures were against it. So he said, "If that's what you want, then we'll not be on your property. I *will* be using the access road though to go onto the government property to search. But I'll be sure to stay off your land. And I would appreciate it if you'd at least not send the dog to the pound if you find him." He didn't wait for a reply, but quickly turned from the doorway and walked to his tractor. As he was starting to pull away, Mr. Arborcide came out of the doorway and yelled, "You make sure to stay off my land, Horst."

Just what is in this man's craw? Mr. Horst wondered.

When Mr. Horst knocked at the door, Mr. Arborcide had only been at the house a couple of minutes. He had come home from town expecting to find his boys there ready to work. Not finding them, he said to himself, "Them two is good for nothin'. Never around when we got work to git done. I'm gonna give 'em a thrashin' when I find 'em." The irritation with his sons was part of the reason for Mr. Arborcide's foul disposition toward Mr. Horst, but not all of it. Mr. Arborcide distrusted his neighbor. Whenever he saw him, something like this went through his mind: *The man is religious, and if he gets wind of what we've been doin' at our mill, he'll turn us in without thinkin' twice.* Consequently, Mr. Arborcide, who would never have thought about throwing anyone off his trail by being nice to them, got gruff with Mr. Horst.

After getting rid of Mr. Horst, he went into the kitchen and picked up one of the portable radios they kept on the counter. He pushed the transmit button and said, "Buzz? Chop? If you boys is listenin', you better talk to me." Some static came from the speaker, and then he heard Chop's voice. "Pa, we's at the mill, and you won't believe what we got. Git yerself over here. There's a present waitin' for you."

Mr. Arborcide knew the boys were just fooling around, and had probably been spending money on something they shouldn't have. He radioed, "I ain't got time for yer foolishness. Now you two git back here, *pronto*. We got work to git done."

Buzz got on the radio next and said, "Pa, we ain't foolin' around. You just git yerself over here, now. This is important. We's turnin' off these radios until you git here. So come on."

Mr. Arborcide didn't like having his own boys demand things of him. But he couldn't raise them on the radio and would have to go find them if he wanted to get any work done today. He walked out to the pole shed, started up his 4x4, and headed over to the mill. The Arborcides didn't have a road leading to the mill, but there was a sort of overgrown path. They tried not to bring a truck through the area often, so it would not look like a road that led somewhere. Mr. Arborcide went up the path through the woods toward the mill. When he got to the white pines, he maneuvered the truck through the small gap in the trees where they went in and out with the flatbed. He pulled on through the camouflage netting up to the mill. There he saw his boys standing with wide grins on their faces.

As he got out of the truck, he said, "I'm gonna thrash you both. What do you mean givin' me orders like that?"

Before he could say another word, Buzz pulled the crooked stick from behind his back and smacked the ground with it. Some kind of thorny tree sprang out of the ground. The boys stepped back beaming. Mr. Arborcide stopped in his tracks wondering what kind of trick the boys were playing on him.

"Don't you two be playin' with me. I'm not in the mood for it."

Chop said, "We ain't playin', Pa. This here's some kind of magic stick. It grows trees."

"Magic stick that grows trees. Have you boys been gettin' into my moonshine?"

"Listen Pa, with this here stick we can grow trees like they was dandelions. We can make a fortune off this mill of ours," Buzz said. "Watch." He took the stick and started whacking the small tree that had just appeared. Each time he struck it the tree shot up higher and grew larger in diameter. Mr. Arborcide stood watching in disbelief.

"What kind of trick you playin' on me boy?"

"It ain't no trick, Pa," Buzz said. "At least it ain't one we're pullin' on you. We seen these kids usin' this thing in the forest yesterday. And today we got it away from 'em. We knew you'd want it."

Mr. Arborcide stood there trying to figure out what his boys were trying to pull over on him. Then he clued in to what Buzz had said and asked gruffly, "Did you say you took this stick from somebody? Where'd you git it?"

Buzz rattled off, "We saw these kids usin' it yesterday in the National Forest. It was them Alder kids . . . you know . . . the fool that almost wrecked us with that load of firewood. Well we been watchin' their house today and seen 'em go over to the Mennonites right next to our place. When they was in the back field with the stick, I sent Grinder to get it. Now *we* got it. And since nobody knows Grinder's ours, we're in business."

"You two must have mush between yer ears," Mr. Arborcide said. "You know who was just at our front door wantin' permission to walk around on our place? Do ya? It was that Horst fella. Seems they have a dog . . . followed Grinder, and now they's lookin' for it." Mr. Arborcide glared at the two boys. They looked at each other with questioning faces. They were wondering whether they should tell their Pa they had that dog penned up right here at the mill. He would find out about it sooner or later, and besides, they didn't know what to do now that people were following them. They needed their Pa's advice. Chop was the first to speak.

"Pa, we got that dog they's lookin' for. Got him penned up out back. We didn't think about them searchin' on our place for him."

Mr. Arborcide shook his head then raised both fists in the air. He let out a big growl and said, "You dimwits.

'Didn't think about them searchin' for him'? Do you think people just forgets about a dog when it runs off? Where is it? Let me see him."

They walked behind the mill over to a large packing crate made out of rough cut boards with narrow slatted openings cut in its sides. Earlier, Buzz had dragged an unconscious Amos up to the mill, put a muzzle over his snout, and then locked him inside the packing crate. When Chop had arrived at the mill, Amos was just starting to revive. He had tried to let out a bark as Buzz showed Chop the crate, but the muzzle did its job well.

As Mr. Arborcide now looked into the crate, Amos recognized his face. All the bad people he'd encountered this week were together. The old man recognized Amos, too. He poked a stick in at Amos and prodded him hard a few times to make him hurt. "That's the mutt what chased me to my truck over at Showalter's. You don't look so dangerous now." Seeing how Grinder had taken care of Amos, made Mr. Arborcide less angry with his boys about all the trouble they had stirred up. The old man had felt ashamed of running to his truck at the airfield, but The Grinder had given this dog "what for." Mr. Arborcide was proud of the way Buzz had trained Grinder. He looked at the gash on Amos' neck and asked, "Did The Grinder do that to him?"

"Yeh, Pa," Buzz answered.

"He don't look all that much hurt to me," Mr. Arborcide said mockingly. "Horst acted like he was all tore up . . . like he's gonna die if they couldn't git on our property to find him," the old man continued.

Buzz saw that his Pa was less angry at him and his brother. He decided to keep this going and said, "You'd a been proud of The Grinder, Pa—the way he handled this one."

"That's good. The no-account-dog's got no business chasin' after me or The Grinder. Now we gotta figure out how to git rid of him without stirring things up any more around here. You boys was careless today. Could have had our whole operation discovered."

Chop said, "But, Pa, what about the stick? We just had to git it. We can make all kinds of money with it."

The old man, remembering the stick, held out his hand. Buzz gave it to him. "How's this thing work?" he asked.

"You just hit the ground with it and a tree'll pop up, or hit a tree and it'll grow bigger. Just like we showed you, Pa," Chop said.

Mr. Arborcide swung the stick onto the ground and another thorny tree sprang up. "Dang. If that don't just beat all. I never seen anything like it. What kinda tree is that anyway? It's all thorny."

"I don't know, Pa," said Buzz.

"Well, if that's all it'll grow, it ain't much of a magic stick. We need some good hardwoods to sell to our dealer—not thorn bushes."

"Seems like them kids were growin' trees that wasn't thorny. I couldn't see *real* good, but I don't think they

158 | *Marty A. Bullis*

were like this one. Maybe the more you use it the better it'll work," Buzz told him.

"We ain't got time to find out right now," said their Pa looking at both of them. "That Horst fella said he was going to start snoopin' on the government land around our place. We need to get down there and keep an eye on him. And, while we're watchin' him we need to figure out what to do with this dog. He can't stay here. We may just have to *dis-pose* of him," he said eerily.

Amos was watching Mr. Arborcide as he said this last sentence. He didn't like the way he said it, so he scowled at him. There was something evil in the man's voice. He growled a long muffled growl through the muzzle. The Arborcides all laughed at him and went back around to the other side of the shed. Grinder, who had been sitting and guarding the crate, looked at Amos and growled as if saying, "Be quiet or I'll tear into you again."

Without putting it back in its case, Buzz Arborcide laid the magic tree wand in the gun rack of the truck. He closed the door and walked over to his ATV. His father and brother had already started down the hill through the woods to the house. Grinder came around the mill to see him off. Buzz petted the dog and said, "You did real fine today, boy. *Real* fine. Now, I want you to stay and guard the mill. If anybody comes snoopin', you know what to do." He started the ATV and drove off. There were still a few hours of daylight left, when people might be searching for Amos. The Grinder sat on alert.

Amos lay in the crate wanting to lick his wounds, but he couldn't get his tongue past the muzzle. As the sun was setting, he felt cold and sore. His neck and right hind leg were throbbing, and he was still losing some blood from the gashes. But worse than these pains, was the sense that he'd let Matty down. He hadn't gotten the stick back and had been caught by these people.

He curled up as best he could, given his pains, and waited for the last rays of light to fade around him. As he drifted off into a fitful sleep, the forest seemed darker than he'd ever seen it before.

TIME TO CONFESS

EVERYONE WAS ASTONISHED when Mr. Horst returned home without obtaining Mr. Arborcide's permission to search his woods. Mr. Alder said, "I can't believe that guy. He's just plain evil."

Mrs. Alder was shocked that this had come out of her husband's mouth, especially in front of people they hardly knew. She said, "Ben Alder, think about what you're saying. It just isn't Christian. Mr. Arborcide certainly isn't very nice. But we shouldn't go around calling people *evil*."

Mr. Horst noticed the tension between Mrs. Alder and her husband. He stepped in and said, "I'll be the first to admit my neighbor's a hard man to get along with, but we've got to respect his right not to have people on his property."

Mr. Alder now felt a little embarrassed by his remarks. He said, "I apologize to you all. Especially to you, Matty and Ryker. It's just that every encounter we've had with this man has been bad news. I'm not sorry we won't be on his land—possibly running into him. I can't say I'd act very 'Christian' to him, given the way he treated the kids the other day." He paused for a moment, then said, "I just hope we can find Amos, wherever he is."

"We *will* find him," said Mr. Horst, who had already developed a plan. The ladies were going to stay at the house and look after Matty, while Mr. Horst, Mr. Alder, and Ryker searched for Amos. Matty wasn't happy about this arrangement. Her head had started to feel much better while Mr. Horst was gone and she wanted to help search for Amos.

"Mom, I need to go. Amos was hurt trying to protect *me*," she said.

But her mother insisted she stay put for a while. Mrs. Alder wasn't very happy about Ryker going along either. Mr. Alder told her he thought Amos would come to Ryker more quickly than to him, so she reluctantly agreed to let Ryker go. She had one stipulation though: Ryker had to remain with Mr. Alder all the time—no running off alone. Ryker thought this was okay, as long as he was allowed to go. With this settled the guys left the house and headed up to the barn.

On the way Mr. Horst asked Mr. Alder if he and Ryker would be able to ride a horse together. "No problem. We can handle that. We ride them at my in-law's farm whenever we're there," he answered.

Mr. Horst told them, "I've got Dunlap, who was trained as a saddle horse before I switched him to pulling buggies, and Deborah, a nice five-year-old chestnut mare. Real strong gal. Be just right for the two of you. She's named after the woman judge in the Old Testament. She and Dunlap are quite a pair. I'll get 'em saddled up and we'll have a look in the woods."

Mr. Horst went to the tack room and got a couple of oat bags and bridles. They went to the field, rounded up the horses, and led them back to the tack room where they saddled them. Mr. Alder and Ryker saddled the mare by themselves and Mr. Horst checked the cinch to make sure everything was secure. Within twenty minutes they were off to look for Amos. It was getting late in the afternoon and the sun would soon be behind the mountains to the west. They needed to hurry.

Riding the horses hard, they got to the edge of the woods quickly. Ryker was mounted behind his dad and holding on tightly. He was sitting on part of the saddle blanket (like he did at his Nana's). The woods were thick with underbrush and dead leaves, so they needed to walk the horses along slowly. Leaves crunched and sticks snapped under the heavy weight of Dunlap and Deborah. Mr. Horst guided them up the hill, following the direction Amos had taken earlier. They went as far as they could before running into Mr. Arborcide's "No Trespassing" signs. Blood drops here and there led on past the farm's boundary line.

Mr. Horst said, "We can ride around the property line and call Amos." He directed his horse southward along the line. Mr. Alder and Ryker followed on the chestnut mare.

"Ryker, it's your job to call Amos," his dad told him. "I need to watch for holes and rocks. You keep up the calling."

"I'm on it, Dad," Ryker said.

They rode southward for about twenty minutes along the hilly terrain to the back corner of the Arborcide farm. Mr. Horst's and Mr. Arborcide's properties butted up to the government land here. Mr. Horst said, "Ben, we can head west along the back of Arborcide's place, through the National Forest. We're allowed to take the horses through there." They followed the back of the property line a long way until it started curving northward. It was marked with yellow "No Trespassing" signs every 20 feet. The sun was behind the higher mountains to the west when they got around a curve and were heading due north. Ryker had been calling Amos the whole time without any sight or sound of him. They went north along the far side of the Arborcide farm until they came to the first fire road.

"I'm sorry, Ben, Ryker. I sure had hoped we'd find something. We can head along this road to the state road, then take that back to the house. It's getting late and we need to get back before dark. I don't want any cars running up on us from behind us. I didn't think to bring along any lights."

Mr. Alder said, "Sounds like the best thing to do. We'll have to try again first thing in the morning. I just hope Amos isn't injured badly. He's taken care of himself in the woods before. Just have to trust he can get along tonight."

Ryker's heart sank as he listened to his father. He was really worried about Amos. What if that other dog had hurt him more? Maybe he was dying. They wouldn't find out tonight. Wasn't there something else they could do?

Dunlap was in the lead as they headed down the fire access road. The horses made the turn onto the state road and hadn't gone far when they heard the loud whine of ATVs coming up behind them. It spooked them a little. The Arborcide boys were speeding toward them with headlights blazing. Mr. Horst, with some effort, side-stepped Dunlap to the edge of the road and Mr. Alder did the same with Deborah.

The Arborcide boys had been keeping a lookout for Mr. Horst that afternoon. They hadn't seen him go into the woods on horseback and didn't know where he was until they saw him on the road with Mr. Alder. Their father had told them, "Git up there and find out if them snoopers has seen anything." Buzz and Chop roared up to the horses in a cloud of gravel and dust, slamming on their brakes at the last instant.

"Hey, Horst," Buzz yelled in a sneering tone. "Just came to see if you'd found that dog. We ain't seen hide nor hair of him on our place. Pa tells me he may have lost some of his hide."

"No, we haven't found him," Mr. Horst replied curtly.

Buzz smiled and said, "That's too bad."

Chop snickered at his brother's remark. Then he looked at Mr. Alder and said, "I know you. Your name's Alder, ain't it?"

"Yes. I don't think I know you, though," Mr. Alder answered. Ben Alder wasn't liking the tone these boys were using with him or Mr. Horst, and was trying not to get angry.

"My brother here tells me you nearly made him and Pa wreck one day by runnin' like a fool on the road. Said you was wearin' one of them flashin' lights, like goes on bicycles." Now it was Buzz's turn to snicker at his brother's remark.

"Well, you tell your Pa . . . and this goes for both of you as well . . . that if you try something like that again, I'll ask my friend Sheriff Goode to pay you a visit. He'll be bringing an arrest warrant with him for attempted assault with a vehicle." Mr. Alder had had enough of the Arborcides today, and he wasn't going to be harassed.

When the Arborcide boys heard that the sheriff was a friend of Mr. Alder, it got their attention. They decided to back off. Although they were mean-natured and wanted to keep baiting Mr. Alder, they were smart enough to know they didn't need the attention of the local law enforcement drawn to them.

Buzz said, "All right, Alder, my brother's got a big mouth. He didn't mean nothin' by it. You all go on and git off our property. We'll keep a look out for that dog of yers."

Mr. Alder didn't like being told what to do by these fellas. He said, "Last time I heard, this road was a public right-of-way into the National Forest, so we'll move along when our business is finished." He paused, thinking for a moment, and asked, "What makes you think that was *my* dog, anyway?"

"Pa told us it was some girl's who was visiting Horst here," he said pointing to Mr. Horst. "And since you was out searchin' with him, I figured it was yer animal."

Both Mr. Alder and Mr. Horst were suspicious of this explanation, but couldn't find any reason to push the matter further. They needed to get home soon. So they let it drop and started moving away without saying anything further. When they had gone about twenty-five feet, Buzz yelled to them, "You all have a *nice* night." He drew out the word "nice," saying it in a drippy-sweet way. Buzz may have been afraid of Sheriff Goode, but that wasn't enough to suppress his rudeness for long.

By the time the searchers arrived home, the sun was down and darkness was gathering itself around the farm. The ladies heard them ride up in front of the house and ran out to see if they'd found Amos. Matty began to cry again when she saw that Amos wasn't with them. Her mother once more tried to comfort her, but with no success.

Mr. Alder and Mr. Horst took care of the horses and came back to the house, where the ladies and children were waiting for them. Everyone was feeling pretty low. The Horsts felt badly about having something like this happen to their guests. Matty and Ryker were sick about losing the magic tree wand, but even more, they were worried about Amos. They would give up anything, even the tree wand if they still had it, to get him back. Amos was their best friend.

Mr. and Mrs. Alder drove the children home in silence that evening. When they arrived, Matty and Ryker didn't want to go to bed. How could they, with Amos lost and hurting? He wouldn't give up on *them*. Their mom and dad convinced them that the best way to help Amos would be to get rested up. Tomorrow they would need all their strength to search for him. Reluctantly, Matty and Ryker agreed to at least get ready for bed and lie down, but they weren't promising that they could sleep—or anything like that.

Ryker lay in bed thinking, *If only I'd been quicker or stronger, I could have helped Amos. King Arthur would have killed that dog with one stab of his sword.* He lay in bed and prayed that he would grow bigger and stronger soon.

Matty was thinking only about Amos. She thought, *If it hadn't been for the stick, he never would have gotten hurt or run off after that dog. He knew the stick was important to me and was trying to get it back.* She felt worse and worse as she thought about what happened at the farm. Slowly, sleepiness started to get the best of her. As her eyelids got heavier, she was thinking about the events of the week. She and Ryker had had such adventures with the stick—so many exciting things had happened. But then she began to remember the bad things that had also happened. Replaying in her mind the troubling events of the week, she wondered how they could be connected with the appearance of the stick. Soon she was sleeping fitfully and having wild dreams. Next to her bed, one of Amos' rawhides lay on the floor along with her backpack, which was empty tonight.

Thursday morning the entire Alder household rose early to get going on the search for Amos. Mrs. Alder planned to cook a full breakfast with oatmeal, scrambled eggs, bacon, and fruit. The family would probably be in for a long day of searching, and the big meal would help sustain them.

While things were cooking, Mr. Alder decided to pull out all the stops and enlist the help of his friends. He called Bob Meyer at home and told him the situation. Bob said, "I can get over to your place about 9 A.M., and I'll bring all the search equipment I can lay my hands on." Ranger Bob loved the kids, and he knew how much Amos loved them. He was going to do everything he could to find that pup.

Next thing, Mr. Alder called the Showalters' home. Mrs. Showalter answered the phone and listened to Mr. Alder tell her about Wednesday's troubles. He asked if Mr. Showalter might have time to fly over and have a look around. She put Mr. Showalter on the phone and he told Mr. Alder that he had some aerial spraying he had to get done early that morning, but after that was finished he'd make sure to fly over. "It might be hard to spot him," he said, "but we'll give it a whirl." When Mr. Showalter heard that Bob Meyer would be searching, he said he would call him to coordinate things. The Showalters often did aerial spraying for the Forest Service, and knew how to communicate with the rangers by radio from the air.

Mr. Alder made two other calls: one to the Horsts, and one to Miss Anne and Miss Sue. He told them about the help that was coming and when they would be ready. Starting a little after 9 A.M. was good for the Horsts. It would let them get their morning farm work completed. Miss Anne and Miss Sue told Mr. Alder they couldn't make it until a little later, but that when they got there they'd have a big surprise of their own to aid the search.

Mr. Alder got off the phone and told the family about the help that was coming. "Wow!" Matty exclaimed. "Can you believe what good friends they are to come and help just like that?"

"Yes they are," Mrs. Alder told her. "And you know what? I think they all love our little guy as much as we do."

Mr. Alder looked around at everyone and said, "If we're going to find our boy, we'd better fill up on breakfast and get our stuff together. Once Bob gets here, we can start right out."

They heartily ate the good food Mrs. Alder had prepared, now having a sense of hope that with all their friends' help they would be able to find Amos. After breakfast, the children and Mr. Alder cleaned up the dishes, then joined Mrs. Alder in getting dressed for the day. Everyone put on their hiking gear again and packed backpacks with binoculars (these could come in handy looking for Amos). Mrs. Alder returned to the kitchen to prepare a stack of tuna fish sandwiches. Matty and Ryker came down from their rooms to the kitchen and got together bags of trail-mix, peanut butter crackers, and bottles of sports drink. These high-energy foods were just what they were going to need through the day.

It was still before 8 A.M. and the Alders had everything ready. To wait more than an hour seemed an eternity to them all, but the plans were set. Matty and Ryker went outside on the front porch to look for Ranger Bob while Mr. and Mrs. Alder spent some time doing household chores. The two friends sat in the large porch swing talking about all the adventures they'd had with Amos. He was the best dog they'd ever seen, both agreed.

"Matty, what are we gonna do if Amos is . . . you know . . . dead?" Ryker asked.

"I just know he's not dead. I can't tell you why, but I have a sense about it. We're going to find him today."

"But what if we don't? All kinds of bad stuff has been happening since we found that magic tree wand. Amos has gotten hurt twice this week protecting us, and both times we had the wand with us. He rushed off to get it back for *us*. What if he died trying to get it?"

Matty was feeling guilty as Ryker said this. She snapped at him, "I don't *know* Ryker. It's not *my* fault he ran off. I didn't do anything wrong."

Ryker had been feeling guilty himself since yesterday. Losing one of his best friends started him thinking. *If it hadn't been for that magic wand, Amos would be okay and with them right now.* And *this* started him to thinking about having lied to their parents about the stick, or at least not having told them the whole truth about it. Now he felt even guiltier about what had happened—and still might be happening—to Amos. He looked at Matty and said, "You did do something wrong, Matty, and so did I. Maybe we're both responsible for Amos' getting hurt."

"What are you talking about, Ryker?" she asked. Matty was very perplexed by what Ryker had said.

"I'm saying that maybe if we hadn't lied to Mom and Dad about the magic wand, maybe Amos wouldn't be in the spot he's in."

Matty hadn't thought about it this way before. She started feeling guiltier than ever. It made her recall all the events of the week with the stick: their bikes being stolen, hitchhiking with the Horsts, trees in Mr. Arborcide's field, Amos getting hurt by the tree thieves, and the mean dog hurting Amos and causing him to run off. Perhaps none of it would have happened if they'd never found the magic wand? Or what if they'd told their parents? Would it have made any difference in how things had turned out? She and Ryker were silent for a little while. They were both staring straight ahead as the swing rocked back and forth.

Matty finally said, "Ryker, I don't like what you said one bit." She paused, then continued, "But then I started thinking about it. What if you're right? What if we had let Mom and Dad in on our secret? I don't know how it would have changed things, but if it would have kept Amos from getting hurt . . . ? I just don't know. I feel all confused inside."

"Well, I think we need to tell 'em," Ryker decided. "They need to know why Amos was so determined to run off and didn't listen to anyone. I don't know why, but I think we ought to. I'm all confused inside too."

Matty thought about this for a while, and then reluctantly agreed. She didn't like it much. It meant telling their parents they'd been keeping things from them—and lying. Matty didn't like getting in trouble. But Amos was in trouble! She didn't know why, but it seemed telling the truth might help him—might set some things straight.

"All right, Ryker. It may mean we're grounded for eternity or something like that, but I think you're right. Let's go talk to them."

The two friends walked inside and found their mom in the kitchen. Ryker went to find their dad, while Matty told their mom they had something they needed to tell them together. The guys came into the kitchen and found Matty and Mrs. Alder sitting down silently at the breakfast nook. They took a seat and everyone looked around at each other. The children were feeling even *more* guilty now and kept diverting their eyes from their parents' gazes.

Mr. Alder finally asked, "Okay, what's going on? Seems pretty important since we're having a family meeting."

The children looked at each other and continued to be silent, fearing to speak.

"We're all ears," Mrs. Alder said, hoping to coax them along.

Ryker finally burst out, "We lied to you about something, and it may be important."

"Lied? . . . About what?" Mrs. Alder asked quietly.

"About Matty's stick," he blurted.

Matty was looking sheepishly at the placemat in front of her. She was starting to feel sick again. *Maybe this confession stuff isn't the right thing to do*, she thought.

"Matty, what's this all about?" Mr. Alder asked gently.

She hesitated for a moment, and then everything flooded out. "Our crooked stick—it's a magic tree wand. We grew trees with it. *That's* why Amos tried to get it back from the mean dog. He knew it meant a lot to us. And we lied about it because we were afraid everyone would want to take it from us."

She was almost panting now. Her father told her to slow down and tell them slowly. Taking a deep breath, she started to recount everything they knew about the magic tree wand. Then she told them all the lies of the week: making up the story about spiders when they'd seen the first fir tree; keeping quiet about the fir tree when they'd heard the radio report; lying about what they'd been doing during their Holmes and Watson adventure; not telling anyone about where the trees in Mr. Arborcide's field had *really* come from; and lying about where they'd gotten the saplings they planted in the forest. All of this spilled out like a waterfall once she started. When Matty finished telling all of this, she dropped her forehead to the table and started to cry. Ryker looked his sister and felt badly for her, but he was glad it was all out in the open—what a relief!

Mr. and Mrs. Alder didn't know what to make of the story. At first they couldn't believe that the stick the kids had found could really "grow trees." It seemed ridiculous. And all the lying they said they'd done really shocked them. Their kids had never lied like *this* before. They sat quietly, attempting to think this through.

Finally Mr. Alder put his arm around Matty and asked, "So, Matty, you mean to tell me that this crooked stick is somehow magical and *really* did all these strange things?"

She picked her head up, eyes still tearing, and said, "Yes, Dad, it's all true. We were so bad about it."

Mrs. Alder spoke up. "I'm starting to believe you, Matty. It's just incredible, though. And the lies, those are incredible too. Why did you and Ryker concoct all of them?"

Ryker said, "We wanted to keep it a secret so we could use it, Mom. We were afraid you wouldn't understand, and that other people would take it away from us. I'm the one who made all those big trees appear out on Route 259, so I should be the one getting in trouble for that."

"I'm not sure what to make of all of this. It seems strange, and I want to believe you. Can you understand that?" asked Mr. Alder.

"Dad, we didn't believe it at first, either. That's why we did all those Holmes and Watson experiments. Remember, Holmes says, 'When you have eliminated all which is impossible, then whatever remains, however improbable, must be the truth.' You taught us that. And the magic tree wand grows trees. We've done it. We grew them in the back yard, in Mr. Arborcide's field, and even in the National Forest, where the thieves had stolen the trees."

Mr. and Mrs. Alder were still amazed, but were really starting to believe their children. Mr. Alder said, "Did you say you grew some in the forest?"

"Yeh, Dad," Ryker answered. "We grew a bunch of them to replace the stolen ones. Right after that Amos got hurt . . . remember?"

"Yes, I remember." Mr. Alder looked out the window deep in thought. *Could there be a connection between those thieves and the loss of the stick?* he wondered. He didn't say anything about this in front of the children.

"What do you two think we should do about all these lies this week?" asked Mrs. Alder.

Matty and Ryker looked at one another and realized it was time to reap the consequences of their actions. Matty started, "I don't know, Mom, I'm not sure what got into me. I'm the one that started it all."

"I'm not sure what got into you, either," Mrs. Alder said. "Seems like this magic wand certainly spun you for a loop in a lot of ways."

Ryker said, "It sure did."

They all paused to think things over some more. Mr. Alder spoke first and said, "We want you to think about this for a while. We'll need to work out some way to make up for all of this. But right now we have other matters to attend to. We've got a friend who is lost in the woods, and he needs all of us trying to find him. Ranger Bob should be here in a few minutes. I think we'll need to sit down and have a long talk with him about this magical stick. That'll have to wait until after we get Amos back."

"Before we go, I want to tell you that I am glad you told us all this on your own," said Mrs. Alder. "I'm sure it wasn't easy to get up the courage to tell us about these things. You will need to do something to set things right, but we'll figure that out."

Matty was feeling a little relieved but was still unsure for the most part. She asked her mom, "Do you forgive me, Mom? Dad?"

"We forgive you both," Mr. and Mrs. Alder said together.

"You still love us?" Ryker asked energetically.

"Yes, we do," their parents said, again in unison.

"But you're still gonna have to do some penance, young man." Mr. Alder said. "Now, you two finish getting ready. We've got hard work to do today."

The children went upstairs to get their things. Mrs. and Mr. Alder sat at the table trying to make sense of all the mysterious things they'd heard this morning. They didn't seem so strange in light of how the week had turned out. "What a spring break!" Mrs. Alder sighed.

GRINDING THE GRINDER

RANGER BOB PULLED INTO THE DRIVEWAY just after 9 A.M. The Alders were raring to go and rushed out of the house with their gear. Stepping out of his truck, Ranger Bob said cheerfully, "Hey, is anybody available to be on a search and rescue squad?" He was dressed in his ranger's uniform and was wearing the gun the Alders had seen for the first time on Tuesday.

The kids rushed him with big hugs and said, "We are! Let's get going."

Mr. Alder thanked Bob for coming. Mrs. Alder, feeling a little teary said, "Bob, you're a gem. I know you've got plenty to do. Thanks for taking the time to help us."

"Wouldn't miss it for the world. Besides, I hear we're searching on Forest Service land. As far as I'm concerned, it's just like I was at the office. We look for lost hikers all the time . . . though I can't say as I've ever been on a dog hunt." The ranger smiled a great big smile. He had lifted the kids into the air and was still holding them with their arms and legs dangling. He shook them a little and said, "Come on, Junior Rangers. We've got somebody lost in our forest and we've got to find him. Load up!" He put them back on their feet and they headed for his truck. Mr. and Mrs. Alder followed their lead and got in the truck carrying all the gear. Bob didn't waste any time getting the truck moving toward the Horst's farm.

Ryker and Matty were sitting up front with Bob again while their parents were in the back seat. Mr. Alder looked into the cargo area of the big SUV and asked Bob what all the equipment was. He told him he'd brought everything but the kitchen sink: climbing gear, winches, ropes, waders . . . anything he could think of.

"I've also got something back there that's *top secret*," he said as he smiled at the kids.

Ryker squinted his eyes, looked at Ranger Bob and said in 007 fashion, "You can inform me of the secret equipment, Ranger. The name's Alder . . . *Ryker* Alder."

Matty looked back at her parents and rolled her eyes. She said, "He's hopeless!"

Ranger Bob had a different reaction. He let out a good-natured loud laugh and then said, "I knew I'd get your attention with that one . . . Secret Agent Alder. I was just pulling your leg about the 'Top Secret' stuff, but I *do* have some pretty fancy new gear to put to use. We're experimenting with a new global positioning system at the station—a GPS. It's got a handheld receiver that takes the signal from a satellite and tells you your position. We can feed those coordinates into a portable computer that has maps of the National Forest. It shows you where you're hiking and what kind of terrain is around. Pretty hot stuff for an ole Ranger like me, huh?"

Ranger Bob laughed his deep wonderful laugh again. Everybody felt a bit lighter around him. Ryker and Matty were amazed at all this gadgetry. Ranger Bob seemed to be an expert at search and rescue. Surely they would be able to find Amos with him along.

The SUV turned into the Horst's lane and they all saw Mr. Horst with Dunlap and Deborah, saddled up and ready to go. The truck stopped in front of the house and everyone got out. Mrs. Horst came from the backyard to greet them.

"Hello, folks," Mr. Horst said. "Hello, Mr. Meyer. The Alders told me you were coming."

"Good morning Mr. Horst . . . Mrs. Horst," Bob said, nodding to each in turn. "Good to see you both again. And please, call me Bob."

The Horsts had often seen Bob as he was traveling to the ranger's station and had spoken to him a few times. But the Horsts, not wishing to become involved in government matters, hadn't gone out of their way to get to know Bob. For his part, Ranger Bob understood only a little about the Horst's religious beliefs. What he did know led him to believe it might be better if he didn't wander around their property with a gun today. So he said to Mr. Horst, "I think it'll be best if I start searching from the fire access road near the Arborcide place and work my way back over this way. If you and Ben search in the opposite direction, we can cover the ground more quickly. Then we can expand our search on into the forest if we need to. I've got radios so we can keep in touch."

"That sounds like a good plan to me . . . Bob," Mr. Horst said, hesitantly using the ranger's first name.

Bob unpacked a handheld radio and showed Mr. Alder how to use it. Then he announced, "Okay. I'm off. I'll meet you in the forest."

Ryker listened to all the plans, and there was no mention of what *he* was supposed to do. He was dying to see the fancy equipment Ranger Bob had with him. *And besides,* he thought, *Ranger Bob needs a partner.* So he yelled out, "Wait a minute. Don't you need some help?"

Ranger Bob stopped and said, "Now, I don't know about that. You'd better see what your mom and dad think."

Ryker stared at his parents with begging eyes. Mr. and Mrs. Alder looked at one another. They were thinking that Ryker might get in Bob's way; but they didn't want to say this in front of everyone. Bob stepped in and said, "I'll watch after him if he wants to come. He's experienced in the woods. It won't be a problem."

Mrs. Alder said, "All right, Ryker, but you listen closely to Bob."

"What about *me?*" Matty demanded. "I don't want to just stay here."

"Why don't you ride with me on Deborah?" Mr. Alder asked her. He was thinking that Bob certainly didn't need to be looking after *both* of their children today. He turned to his wife and said, "Karen, I'll take care of Matty. We'll need you and Mrs. Horst to bring Sue and Anne along when they come. They've got some kind of surprise they say will help us today. I'm not sure what it is. Could be interesting . . . knowing them."

Mrs. Alder sighed deeply and said, "Once again, the women are left behind. All right Ben Alder, *we'll* come along with Sue and Anne. But you two," she said to her husband and Ranger Bob, "watch out for my babies." Turning to Matty she said, "And *you*, Miss Alder, hold on tightly to your father."

Karen Alder knew the kids would be miserable if they couldn't help search for Amos. "They're very experienced in the forest," she tried to reassure herself, "but they're still my babies." Even her great trust of her husband and Bob Meyers wasn't going to stop her from worrying at least a little about the children.

Ranger Bob said, "Karen, I've got a radio for you as well." He handed it to her and showed her how to use it. With everything settled, Ranger Bob and Ryker headed off to the access road while Mr. Horst, Mr. Alder, and Matty rode off toward the forest. The ladies stood by watching them leave.

A few minutes later, Ranger Bob pulled the truck off the access road into the woods. Ryker said, "How far can we take your new truck into the forest? Won't we get stuck?"

"Oh, I'm not going far. We could get stuck, but that's not why I'm stopping. Real reason is that I don't want to damage the land too much. We'd be running over a lot of stuff that you're not supposed to run over with a vehicle around here. We're hoofin' it on foot today. You up for it?"

"Sure, I'm up for it. I won't slow you down."

They parked the truck, got out, and went back to the rear doors. Bob took out the gear he thought they'd most likely need and that was light enough to carry. He loaded these things in his big backpack and swung it onto his shoulders, cinching the straps and belt down tightly. Then he opened a large aluminum briefcase. Inside were the computer and GPS unit. He pulled them out and turned them on to see if they were working properly. Ryker watched as the computer booted up and displayed a login window. Bob typed in his name and password, then loaded the mapping program. After hooking up the GPS unit, he showed Ryker a small red flashing dot on the map.

"That's us," Ranger Bob said. "When we move, that red dot will move across the map showing us where we're going."

"Wow, that's cool!" Ryker exclaimed. "Can I carry it for you? I'm a good navigator."

"Well I'm not going to leave it on. We'll save the battery power for when we really need it. I'm putting it in sleep mode and storing it in this case that attaches to the backpack belt." Bob showed him a strong nylon case that clipped onto his belt. He put the two pieces of electronic equipment in the case. "Now we're ready. Let's get searching."

They walked southward, away from the access road. The sun was continuing its morning rise and warming the forest floor. Ranger Bob and Ryker were following the same path that had been searched the night before. They were using the same yellow "No Trespassing" signs to guide them. Ryker yelled for Amos frequently. The more steps he took, the more he remembered that the terrain had not seemed so hilly last night. Now that he was going up and down the hills on foot, he realized how steep they were. There was no way he and Ranger Bob could cover the ground as fast as the horses had. He let out a long groan and said, "This is hard work, Ranger Bob."

"You've got *that* right, my friend. Makes you see why hunters bring in those ATVs to haul out their kill. Can you imagine carrying out a dead bear or deer over these hills?"

"I think I'd probably fall over dead along with the bear or deer," Ryker replied, and they laughed together.

"Let's stop and take a break," said Ranger Bob. "I bet you've got some treats by the looks of that backpack."

"Yeh. Mom packed us some good stuff. I'll pull it out." They sat down on a fallen tree, sipped sports drink, and ate peanut butter crackers together. They were in a narrow ravine with a small brook running through it. Above them, at the top of the hill to the east, someone was watching them through a spotting scope.

Mr. Horst and Mr. Alder set out on horseback with Matty soon after Ranger Bob and Ryker had left. Once again, the horses galloped down the tractor path and climbed the hill through the woods. Matty hadn't been in these woods yet and was taking in everything as she rode along behind her father. For some reason that she couldn't understand,

Matty felt a strange sense of peace holding onto her father. It was a feeling she'd had once before, riding in the backseat of the car during a violent thunderstorm as he drove the family safely home. She soaked in the feeling for a moment.

Matty was calling for Amos every few seconds. She wanted him to feel as safe as she did. *There's no sign of him, though,* Matty thought. *If he were around, he'd hear us. Maybe he isn't around. No . . . he couldn't have just disappeared!*

They continued to follow the property line until they came to the back corner. Mr. Horst stopped Dunlap and asked Mr. Alder what he was thinking. "It seems like we'll need to expand our search into the National Forest after we meet up with Bob."

"That's what I was thinking, too."

"But doesn't everything lead to Mr. Arborcide's place, Dad? Can't we sneak over and peak around?" Matty implored.

"That's just not an option, Honey. Mr. Arborcide doesn't want us on his land, and we'd be breaking the law—trespassing."

"But, Dad . . . " she started.

"I know, Matty . . . but we can't . . . that's all there is to it," he said and turned Deborah westward along the back edge of the Arborcides' property. "Keep up your calling though. Maybe Amos will hear you."

Just then Ranger Bob radioed. "Ben? . . . Ben? Come in, Ben."

Mr. Alder unclipped the radio from his belt and said, "I'm here, Bob, what do you need?"

"We're taking a break right now at the bottom of a ravine. We'll start working our way around to you soon. Haven't seen a thing ourselves. What have you found?"

"Nothing, Bob. We'll take a short break, too . . . give the horses a rest, then start your way."

"Good! See you soon. Over."

Mr. Alder put the radio on his belt and helped Matty slide off Deborah. He and Mr. Horst also dismounted and stretched their legs. They ate a few snacks as they stood around looking at the "No Trespassing" signs. Matty kept calling for Amos now and again.

Though Matty couldn't know it, a muzzled Amos heard the faintest whisper of her voice on the wind—so faint that even Grinder didn't hear it. But Amos' ears were attuned to Matty's voice in a special way. He felt revived and tried to bark. The only sound he could manage through the muzzle was a muffled snorting-growl, not loud enough to alarm even The Grinder.

Some time later the two search parties met along the northward curve of the property line. No sign of Amos had turned up, so they discussed what to do next. Ranger Bob suggested both parties head together into the forest a ways and then, splitting up again, double back in the direction from which they'd come. He also said that if they zigzagged a bit on their return path, they'd cover a wider area. The men agreed this was the logical next step.

Bob added, "We'll all have to keep a sharp eye out for *any* sign of Amos: blood, fur, stool, disturbed ground cover. And remember kids . . . we're *gonna* find him."

So after a short break, they headed away from the Arborcides' property into the National Forest. Once again, they were being observed from a distance. The Arborcide boys had made a little rendezvous and were keeping track of the searchers' every move.

The search parties went a distance away from the Arborcide property line into the forest. Soon they were ready to separate again.

On the other side of the county, Mr. Showalter had just finished his last spraying run for the morning. Now he could give a quick flyby over the search area and see if he could help. Two or three, maybe four passes were all he could do before heading back for refueling, but this might help. He knew the Alders were feeling pretty low about Amos' disappearance, and for that matter, he was too. He turned the plane in the direction of the National Forest. It took him about eight minutes to fly to the search area. He gave one pass over the Horst farm and saw Mrs. Alder and Mrs. Horst along with Miss Anne and Miss Sue standing out front. The ladies had just arrived to help. Mr. Showalter noticed they had a large dog with them. It was Beauregard. Mr. Showalter rocked the plane's wings to wave at them and flew on.

When the plane approached the forest, Ranger Bob heard it. He took out his radio, changed to another channel, and radioed Mr. Showalter. "Ground team one to aerial reconnaissance. Come in. Over?"

Mr. Showalter heard this and radioed back, "What's with all this fancy radio lingo today Bob? You gettin' professional on me?"

"Just foolin' with you this morning. Anyway, I'll send up some smoke so you can see where we are." Ryker watched Ranger Bob take something that looked like a soda can out of his backpack. He pulled a tab on top of the canister and bright blue smoke poured out of the hole. Ranger Bob set it down and backed up.

"Can you see that red smoke?" Bob teased. "Or did you leave your glasses at home?"

Mr. Showalter laughed into the radio and said, "Red? I always knew you were colorblind. I see blue smoke and I've got your position. Now tell me what you need." Ryker and Ranger Bob waved as Mr. Showalter flew over them.

"Good, you *do* have your glasses on! Well I really need you to do a flyover along the Arborcides' and Horst's back property line and tell me if you can see anything. The property line runs east-west not too far from us. We haven't spotted Amos."

"I'm heading up higher. I can give you two passes and then I'll have to refuel. It'll take me a little while to get back."

"Whatever you can do, we'll appreciate it. And keep an eye out for Ben, Matty, and Horst. They're southeast of us. . . . Not too far."

Mr. Showalter started his passes over the area at a higher altitude. Meanwhile, Ranger Bob got in touch with the mounted patrol and told them what was going on. They had heard the plane and were waving at Mr. Showalter. On the second pass, he saw them and rocked his wings.

Back at the Horst farm the ladies were walking through the field toward the forest. Mrs. Alder remembered she had the radio. When she turned it on, Ranger Bob was talking about what Mr. Showalter was doing. She radioed, "Hello, you all, this is Search Party Three. We have a special surprise: He's big and furry and will sniff Amos out a mile away."

Matty, Ryker, and Mr. Alder heard this and knew she must be talking about Beauregard. How could he help? Sure, he was a bloodhound, but they'd never seen him track anything.

They didn't know what Mrs. Alder now knew. Miss Anne had explained to the other ladies that Beauregard *could* track Amos. His father was a champion bloodhound who had worked on FBI manhunts. "His dad's a real pro. Could sniff a man out from under that manure pond I imagine," she told them as they passed the barn.

Beauregard had inherited his father's talent, but Miss Anne had raised him to be a pet, not a working dog. Lately, however, she'd been working on his tracking skills at home, and was ready to put his skills to the test. On the way to the farm the ladies had stopped by the Alder home and grabbed one of Amos' toys from the front porch. This would give Beauregard the scent he needed to follow. Sure enough, he'd found Amos' trail in the field. Right now he was leading the ladies toward the woods in pursuit of his friend.

Ranger Bob radioed Mrs. Alder, "Sounds great, Karen. Head on over." He switched channels again to ask Mr. Showalter what he'd seen.

"Bob, I don't see anything where you and Ben are. It'd be hard to spot Amos right off, though. But there *is* something you ought to look at. Northeast of you, maybe three quarters of a mile, something doesn't fit. There's a big pine grove in between some hills . . . and the ground color seems off. Never noticed it flying over here before, but I'm paying closer attention now. Can't quite tell what . . . but something's not kosher. If I've got my bearings right, I think it's federal land. I sprayed this area a couple years ago. Anyway I can't take another look now . . . gotta get some fuel. Be back as soon as I can."

"Thanks John," Ranger Bob radioed. "I'll check into it. Come back ASAP. You're a big help."

Bob thought to himself, *Three quarters of a mile northeast? Now, why does that seem wrong?* He radioed Mr. Alder and told him, "Let's meet up again and go back toward the Arborcide place. I've got a feeling about something."

The Arborcide boys had been listening to all of these conversations on their scanners. They had been trailing the search parties since they'd set out. Buzz had followed

Ryker and Ranger Bob, while Chop had shadowed the mounted party. Dressed in their camouflage hunting gear they'd been able to remain hidden from view. Meanwhile, their father was at the farmhouse, directing things by radio.

When Mr. Arborcide heard Mr. Showalter mention the pine grove, he decided he'd better get closer to the action. He radioed his boys to meet him and drove his pickup near the edge of his property. Buzz and Chop were waiting when he arrived. Beyond a ridge in front of the truck was the place where the search parties had met earlier.

The old man got out and said, "Dang government people! They got an airplane flyin' over our property. Spyin' on us. That's what they's up to. An' Showalter put 'em on to the pine grove. They'll come snoopin' this way for sure."

"What are we gonna do, Pa?" Chop worriedly asked.

"What are we gonna *do*? What do you *think* we're gonna do, you dimwit? We're gonna keep 'em off our land. That's for dang sure." Mr. Arborcide paused for a moment to think things through. He developed a plan on the spot and looked at Buzz. "Boy, where's yer four-wheeler?"

"It's down the hill behind your truck, Pa. I got it hid under some brush."

"Well git on it and git over to the mill. I want you to send The Grinder up to us. We're gonna let him give them people a little reception. Then I want you to load up the equipment onto the flatbed. Use that lift and get it ready to go. We ain't gonna git caught with our pants down."

Buzz ran to his ATV, but he drove it quietly over to the mill so the searchers wouldn't hear it. Grinder, who was on duty, came running to meet him. Buzz told him, "Pa needs you to scare off some people up that way." He pointed in the direction of his father and said, "Go! Find Pa!" Grinder tore off through the woods to find the old man.

Buzz walked under the camouflage to check on Amos. As he approached the crate, he noticed there was a big mess of thorn bushes where they had shown their Pa the stick last night. "Where in tarnation did those come from?" Buzz said to himself. "Dang it if Chop ain't been foolin' around with that stick this morning instead of watchin' those searchers." He saw a whole line of thorny bushes leading around the mill right up to the driver's side door of the flatbed. "I'm gonna give that Chop a shakin' when I git my hands on him," Buzz said. He had to step into the thorns in order to open the truck door, and he got pricked in the process. The crooked stick was in its place in the gun rack. *At least Chop put it back*, he thought. He shut the door and fired up the engine. Then he backed the truck into the mill building and loaded the portable milling machines onto the flatbed. After strapping them down, he covered the load with a tarp. He pulled the truck out of the building. Everything was ready to go in a hurry, if need be.

Buzz walked back over to Amos' crate. He was frustrated with his brother for all these thorn bushes and with Amos because the mill was in jeopardy. The thorn pricks and bites on his leg hurt, and he decided to be mean. He took a stick and started jabbing it into the crate at Amos, who tried to dodge the stabs as best he could. Locked up in this cage, however, there was no getting away.

Suddenly Buzz's radio blared out, "What are you doin', boy? Ain't you got that done yet?"

"I sent Grinder and everything's loaded, Pa. What else do you want?" he said impatiently.

"I want you to quit foolin' around and git on over this way. Grinder's on his way to take care of those meddlers. But if he don't scare 'em off, then me and Chop will go down and give 'em what-for. I want you watchin'. If they try to come on our property, you is gonna have to git the flatbed outta there and burn what's left. That includes that little friend of theirs. You hear?"

"I hear you, Pa. I'll come over and watch for you."

"Good. Come on quick."

Buzz gave Amos one final stab with the stick and said, "Things just might be heatin' up for you, you filthy mutt." He laughed wickedly and then headed away to back up his brother and Pa.

The ladies had made their way up to the spot where Amos' trail went across onto the Arborcide property. Beauregard had been smelling Amos' blood most of the way and was wildly eager to find him. This was his friend's blood he was following. He knew it meant trouble. But the ladies had stopped him at the "No Trespassing" sign, trying to decide what to do next.

Mrs. Alder said, "We'll need to take Beauregard around the property line and see if he picks up Amos' scent coming out somewhere."

Miss Sue had been a no-nonsense kind of woman her whole life. She said, "Do you mean to tell me we've got to tippy-toe around this place when our Amos may be over there?"

"Sue, you know you can't do what you're thinking. Just hush up," Miss Anne scolded her as she tried to restrain Beauregard.

"What if Beauregard was in there?" she asked Miss Anne.

"Then I hope I'd still respect a person's property rights and find a way to recover him without trespassing," Anne said.

Something got into Miss Sue as she listened. She was tired of this Arborcide fella—plum tired. Looking at Beauregard she said, "Where's Amos, Beau? Where's Amos?" The dog was already nearly frenzied, having smelled Amos' blood for so long. Sue's deliberate coaxing sent him over the edge. He pulled so hard against Miss Anne that she couldn't restrain him. He bolted off across the Arborcide property howling like only a bloodhound can, dragging his leash behind.

Miss Anne stood there staring as Beauregard dashed off. What had Miss Sue done to her dog? It was unthinkable. She finally stuttered, "You . . . you . . . It's just not right."

Miss Sue looked at the ladies and said, "Come on, ladies. Somebody's got to be brave enough to save that friend of ours. We'll just have to trust the Lord's Prayer on this one. 'Forgive us our trespasses . . .'" She moved quickly after Beauregard. The other ladies followed, still shocked, but secretly, a little excited too.

Bob and Ryker had joined up with Mr. Horst, Matty, and Mr. Alder. They were heading back to the Arborcides' property line when The Grinder came up on them. As he ran towards them, Matty saw him, and screamed. Grinder was bearing down on the horses to spook them. Deborah and Dunlap stayed steady, even with Matty screaming and the growling dog thundering down the hill with bared teeth. Ranger Bob figured this was the dog that had hurt Amos. He didn't hesitate for an instant. Drawing his gun, he fired one shot.

The bullet passed close by Grinder. Bob was just trying to scare him off. It worked. Grinder had seen Buzz kill things with a gun and he wasn't going to get killed, not today anyway. He turned tail and ran without reaching the search party.

Matty was crying again, but Mr. Alder couldn't hold her because he had to steady Deborah. Ranger Bob said,

"Matty, the dog is running off. We're all right. Watch him run."

"Bob, I don't think that dog's wild. It seemed to be coming at us on purpose. Wild strays dogs don't come rushing at big groups like that," Mr. Alder said.

"Yeh, something's fishy . . . that's for certain. Let's stop a minute and reconnoiter. I need to check on something John told me."

The riders got down and Mr. Alder comforted Matty as Mr. Horst held the horses. Ranger Bob pulled out the computer and GPS system, squatted down on his knees, and checked their location. Ryker stood behind him, watching over his shoulder in awe. He wanted to be a ranger some day. He'd wear a gun and protect people and the forest just like Bob.

"That's it!" Ranger Bob exclaimed. "I knew something was off."

"What have you found, Bob?" Mr. Alder asked.

"When John flew over, he told me there was something that looked funny. Said it was northeast of my position about three-quarters of a mile; *and* he thought he remembered spraying that area for the Forest Service a couple years back. Well, if you go by those "No Trespassing" signs that would be on Arborcides' property. But look here!" The ranger showed everyone the map on the computer screen. The National Forest land was shaded green on the map and their location was marked by the red dot. "Three quarters of a mile over that way *is* federal land. This thing doesn't lie," he said of the computer.

"That means those 'No Trespassing' signs are way inside federal land. Arborcide posted them in the wrong place!"

"Let's quit wasting time then. We've got a dog to find," Mr. Alder told him.

Ryker and Ranger Bob set off fast. Mr. Alder, Matty, and Mr. Horst mounted up and followed. The horses passed Bob and Ryker quickly and headed toward the phony property line. Ranger Bob and Ryker hurried to catch up.

The ladies had heard Ranger Bob's shot just after they'd started chasing Beauregard. "My heavens, what was that about?" Mrs. Horst had asked.

"I don't know, but I think we need to get Beauregard and get off this property," said Mrs. Alder.

"The problem is, we don't know which way he's gone," said Miss Sue.

"And whose fault would that be?" Miss Anne asked. "You suppose you should have given it a little more thought before you incited my dog to run off like that?"

"Oh, let's just concentrate on finding Beauregard and Amos right now. You can chastise me all you want later, Anne." The ladies walked around searching and calling for both Beauregard and Amos.

Buzz had just lain down in the grass next to his Pa and brother who were watching from the top of the hill, when Ranger Bob shot at Grinder. The sight of this made Buzz furious . . . burning mad. Mr. Arborcide and Chop had to hold him in order to keep him from running down the hill after the ranger. Meanwhile, Grinder was running back up the hill toward his master. Buzz said, "That guy tried to kill our dog. Let me go down there and whomp him, Pa."

Mr. Arborcide said with fire in his voice, "You listen to me, boy. We ain't got time for your struttin'. They's comin' and they's gonna be on us in a few minutes. When that yella-bellied dog of yers gets back up here, you take him over and burn everything, including that mutt of theirs. Then you git Grinder and that equipment back to the farm and hide 'em in the barn. Me and Chop's goin' down to head 'em off. Now git!"

Beauregard followed Amos' blood like a roadmap. He really did have his father's instincts. The scent led him straight to the pine grove, which he approached as cautiously as Amos had. He found the place where Amos had been clubbed and two more scents were there, which he'd been smelling along the way—a dog's and man's. Beauregard knew this meant trouble. Dragging his leash, he crept through the camouflage and up to the mill. It looked   deserted, but he smelled something in the air. He knew it was Amos! He moved around the mill and saw his friend locked in the crate. Thorn bushes were growing all around. Beauregard approached even more cautiously, expecting a trap. He sniffed the air for the dog or man. Amos saw him and a burst of adrenaline reenergized him.

Finally, Beauregard crept up to the crate. The two friends greeted each other with sniffs, and Beauregard noticed the muzzle on Amos. He whined at his friend's situation.

The latch on the crate had a stick wedged in it, but no lock. Beauregard knew what to do. This was the same kind of latch they had on the door to their shed at home. He pulled the stick out of the eyelet with his mouth and scraped at the latch bar with his front feet. It required some clawing, but the latch bar finally sprung back and Amos was free.

They weren't out of the woods yet, however. There was still the muzzle to deal with. Luckily for the dogs, this was an old muzzle that Buzz had used for years on dogs he took to the fights. The leather straps wrapping behind Amos' head were old and dry. Beauregard chewed at them for a few minutes and the muzzle dropped from Amos' snout. At last, he was free!

The friends were retreating from the mill before Amos remembered the stick. It was why he'd come there in the first place. He started sniffing about. Where was it? He searched the mill without finding it. Beauregard didn't know what his friend was searching for, so he kept an eye and nose out for the man and dog. Finally, Amos saw the stick resting in the flatbed's gun rack. Buzz had left the driver's door window open. It was the only way in for Amos, and it was pretty high off the ground. Amos wasn't sure he could clear that height with his wounded leg, but he had to try. He took a running start and jumped toward the door. Only his front legs made it into the truck's cab. The rest of his body slammed into the side of the door with a thud. His back legs flailed a moment then dug into the paint, scratching to get a foothold. With his strong forelegs he pulled his body upward. Slowly, inch by inch, he got through the open window. Once inside, he quickly grabbed the stick from the gun rack, jumped down to the ground, and started running. Beauregard had carefully watched all of Amos' movements. As soon as Amos hit the ground running, Beauregard was next to him like a shadow. The escape went nowhere fast, though. For in the pine trees, they ran right into The Grinder and Buzz Arborcide returning to set fire to everything.

When Buzz and Grinder had headed off toward the mill, Mr. Arborcide and Chop scampered down the hill just in time to meet Ranger Bob and the others as they passed the "No Trespassing" signs. He said, "What do you think yer doin'? Get off my land!"

Matty and Ryker glared at Mr. Arborcide. Not only was he mean, but he'd kept them from searching for their hurt friend. Coming face to face with him focused their anger. Ryker yelled at the old man, "It's not your land . . . and we can prove it."

"Ryker, hold your tongue. This is Ranger Bob's business," Mr. Alder told him.

Chop heard this and turned to Ranger Bob saying, "And just why is it your business to be trespassing on private land, Ranger?"

"I'm not trespassing because we're all standing on federal land. These 'No Trespassing' signs have been put up in the wrong place," Bob told them.

"I've been living on this farm ten years and that there is my property line. I ought to know it. Had a friend of mine survey it special. Now, you git off or I'll be callin' the sheriff," said the old man. Arborcide was bluffing at this point. He wasn't sure where his property line ran. And the ranger's questioning of it made him worry.

"Mr. Arborcide, this is a global positioning unit. It'll tell me where I am—give or take five meters—anywhere in the eastern United States. I can show you on the computer just about how far off you've put these signs, but I don't have time now. We've got a wounded animal to find. I would appreciate it if you'd go ahead and call the sheriff. We've got a vicious dog roaming about that he needs to take care of." Bob mentioned the dog to determine if Arborcide was somehow connected with it. The old man's eyes flinched, letting Bob know he *did* know something. Mr. Arborcide composed himself quickly and said, "I will be calling the sheriff and I suspect you'll be going to jail soon enough." The old man and his son turned around and walked ahead of them over the ridge top. They got to their truck just as the searchers came over the rise. Ranger Bob saw the pickup and yelled, "You boys, hold it right there. I want you to get your hands on the hood of that vehicle. *Now!*" Ranger Bob had drawn his gun and was pointing it at the Arborcides.

"What do you want? You good for nothin' government snoop."

"I'm detaining you two. If this is your truck, then you've been illegally driving on federal land. This area is off-limits to motorized vehicles. Place your hands on the hood of the truck." Again he yelled out, "Now!" They had no choice but to do as he said. Ranger Bob quickly hand-cuffed them to the door-handle of the truck and said, "Looks like *you* will be seeing the sheriff today."

Bob turned to the others and said, "Now, let's find that dog."

Just then they heard the sound of Mr. Showalter returning. Bob clicked his radio to the right channel. Mr. Showalter was repeating, "Come in Bob . . . Bob come in."

"This is Bob, John!

"I'm back 'ASAP,' just like you asked. The boys had another plane ready to go, so I jumped in her. Where are you now?"

"Standing next to a pickup, northeast of where I was earlier. We're all together heading to check on that pine grove. Can you give me a bearing?"

"I see you. You're about half-mile south-southwest. Got a couple of hills between you and it. I see an ATV parked over that way now. It wasn't there before."

"Copy that. We're on our way," Bob said to Mr. Showalter. Turning to Ben and Matty he said, "I'm sorry, but I'm gonna have to borrow Deborah. The ATV is probably Buzz's. No telling what he's up to. We better keep the kids back for now until I find out what's going on."

Matty and Mr. Alder got off Deborah. Ranger Bob mounted her and told Mr. Horst to stay with the Alders and follow him at a distance. Bob would radio if everything seemed all right ahead. Having given these instructions, Bob set off for the pine grove as the search party's point-man. Mr. Alder put Matty on Dunlap with Mr. Horst and they all waited a few minutes before following Ranger Bob.

Amidst the pine trees, The Grinder was baring all his teeth at Beauregard and Amos. Buzz Arborcide laughed when he saw them trying to escape. He said to Amos, "So, we have a friend who wants to play too. Grinder, show 'em how we play around here. Sic 'em, boy."

The Grinder jumped into Amos and lashed at him with his sharp claws. Amos dropped the magic wand and was pushed backward by the force of the attack. He wasn't alone this time. Beauregard turned instantly to assist his friend. Bloodhounds aren't born fighters, but when riled they can hold their own—and boy was Beauregard riled! He tore into Grinder's side with a viciousness that would make anybody cringe. This forced Grinder to give up his attack on Amos. Grinder was hurting now . . . something he wasn't used to. All his fighting instincts rose to the surface and he dove toward Beauregard's neck to lock on for a death bite. The bloodhound was quicker than Grinder had anticipated and the death bite missed its target. Instead of Beauregard's neck, The Grinder had bitten his front shoulder.

While the dogs were fighting, Buzz picked up the magic wand and made off for the mill. The important business right now was to get the fire started and the milling equipment back to the barn. Buzz moved the flatbed outside of the pine grove and returned to the mill to douse everything with gasoline. He lit the fuel and dashed back to the dogfight to make sure The Grinder had finished things off. The flames took off like a rocket through the dry pine needles and sawdust of the mill.

Mr. Showalter was flying overhead when the flames shot up. John Showalter radioed the authorities about the fire. He told them to get Jack Walsh's people in the air. Walsh Aircraft operated the only fire fighting planes in the region. Mr. Showalter emphasized, "We've got people on the ground near the fire. It could get bad *real* fast." Jack Walsh took the call from the sheriff's office. His pilots were in the air in minutes.

Next, Mr. Showalter let Ranger Bob know about the fire. Bob had already seen the smoke and Mr. Showalter told him where it was coming from. "Which way's it heading John?" he asked.

"West and north right now. We'd better just hope the winds don't shift and send it toward the farms. You all better head south a good ways and then turn east. Try and outflank it."

Bob radioed Mr. Alder about what was happening. The searchers needed to move as fast as they could south through the National Forest and then turn east. "I'll catch you in a minute," Bob said, riding Deborah hard as he talked on the radio.

Mrs. Alder was listening to all of this and said, "We see the fire, Bob. Are you all in danger?"

"We'll be fine if we keep our heads, Karen. I don't know where you are, but you need to get out of the area. Quickly!" he emphasized.

"We're not far from the fire, Bob. Beauregard's gone that way and we were following him."

"Karen, get out of there. The wind may shift. Beauregard will have to take care of himself."

"Take care of my kids, Bob!" she radioed. She turned to the ladies, who had heard everything, and said, "Come on, we have to get out of here!"

Ranger Bob returned the way he'd come. He caught up to the others not far from the Arborcide's truck. He pulled Deborah up to a quick stop and jumped off. "Ben, get Ryker loaded up and move out. This thing may get ugly. I'll get the Arborcides out in the truck. Now go!"

Mr. Alder wasted no time following Bob's orders. He threw Ryker onto the saddle and jumped on behind him. He told the kids, "You two hold on for all you're worth." Then he said to Mr. Horst, "We've got to get the kids out of here, Nelson. Say a prayer!"

"Fly, Dunlap," Mr. Horst said as he gave the horse a swift kick in his ribs. Dunlap tore through the forest terrain headed south. "Fly, Deborah," Mr. Alder said also. Deborah lit out after Dunlap, moving rapidly and surely through the forest.

Ranger Bob ran full steam to the truck and reached it quickly. He un-cuffed the Arborcides from the door handle one at a time, only to re-cuff their hands behind their backs. He asked them, "Tell me the truth. Do you know anything about this fire?"

"We don't know nothin', you snoop," Mr. Arborcide said. "But I do know we better git outta here."

Ranger Bob sensed they weren't telling him the truth. He said, "You two get up there in the bed of the truck and lie down. You better hope I don't bounce you out of it." When they were lying down and holding on, Bob started the truck and headed north then east toward the fire access road. Because of the terrain, this was the only way the pickup could go. Ranger Bob needed to get ahead of the fire, but it was spreading rapidly and moving to block his escape route.

As the flames exploded into the air, Amos was lunging toward the back of The Grinder's neck. He was giving the dog everything he had left. Grinder wriggled backward violently at this bite, releasing his hold on Beauregard's shoulder. He thrashed wildly, attempting to get Amos off, but there was no losing him. Amos had had enough of being beaten. He was staying in this to the end. Beauregard meanwhile was limping badly from deep muscle tears in his front shoulder. He was still trying to get close enough to help his friend. But a bigger problem grabbed his attention. The man was coming back to help his dog, and now he was carrying a weapon. Beauregard bared his teeth and shuffled to put himself between the man and his friend, who had now succeeded in forcing The Grinder down onto the ground.

The man was coming at them with the crooked stick raised like a club. Beauregard barked wildly at the man as he approached. Buzz dashed forward, swung the stick back, and crashed it into the side of Beauregard's head. The bloodhound careened backwards and fell over dazed. Now the man made his move on Amos, who hadn't seen him yet. Again he swung the stick behind him, and again a mighty blow was delivered, this time onto the middle of Amos' back. Amos was startled, but didn't lose his hold on Grinder. Now he had two enemies and his friend couldn't help him. As the man's second blow was coming down towards him, Amos jumped to the side of Grinder. The blow missed its target, smashing instead onto Grinder's neck. The violent strike hurt the dog so badly that he pulled free of Amos' locked jaws, tearing the back of his neck open in the process. He reeled slightly, turned, and attacked this new foe. The first thing he saw was the stick that had hit him. He jumped at it and with his powerful jaws wrenched it from Buzz's hand, still not realizing it was his master who'd struck him.

Amos recognized the magic wand as Grinder pulled it away from the man. The dog's jaws were locked around the middle of the stick like a vice. It was Matty's stick. Amos dove onto one end of it and clamped his mouth down tightly. Amos started thrashing wildly in order to free the stick from the vicious dog.

Beauregard was back on his feet now and saw his friend seize the stick. He didn't know what was so important about it—but Amos knew, and that was enough for Beauregard. Stumbling forward toward the gyrating motions of the two dogs, he lurched and somehow, miraculously, locked his teeth on the other end. Buzz rushed up behind The Grinder, wanting now to get his hands on the stick. Three canine bodies, each in great pain, wriggled every way possible, and Buzz couldn't touch it. The violent wriggling continued. No dog would let it go. Finally, something snapped.

Amos and Beauregard had both pulled backward in the same direction and at the same instant. The magic tree wand turned to splinters halfway down its length, shattering in The Grinder's mouth. A shower of sparks that lit up the entire pine grove erupted from the broken ends. The light was brighter than the raging fire—so bright that Mr. Showalter had to turn his face away as he flew overhead.

This fierce showering of sparks and light lasted thirty or forty seconds and then quickly faded. When Amos and Beauregard were able once more to open their eyes, they saw before them a tremendous growth of thorny things. These were plants, but like nothing they'd ever seen before. They were primordial, ancient-looking thorn bushes. And stuck in the middle of them were their enemies, Buzz Arborcide and The Grinder. They were still alive, but the enormous thorns on all sides held them suspended off the ground. They couldn't move without being punctured.

The fire was raging and spreading. There was no way to help the man and dog get free—the thicket surrounding them was too complete a barrier. So the two wounded fighters hobbled away from the pine grove toward the Horst farm. Each carried a still-sparking piece of the magic tree wand, and each knew that today his friend had saved his life.

PLANTING MAGIC SEEDLINGS

EVERYONE HAD SEEN the brilliant burst of light. Though it was a pure and warm light, it was also utterly overwhelming, forcing all of them to shield their eyes. And so they did—each one stopping where they were. Ranger Bob slammed on the brakes to the pickup, the ladies froze in their steps, and the horses halted on their own. Mr. Showalter was the only one able to keep his eyes open, but only because he didn't look outside the plane's cockpit. He focused his eyes on the instruments, and flew the plane by them.

No one knew what to say when they could see again. There had been no explosive sound. The light didn't seem to have come from the fire. It was, in a word, inexplicable.

Nobody talked, they simply resumed what they'd been doing before the illumination—fleeing from the fire.

The flames were still growing. Ranger Bob hurried to get back to the Arborcides' farm and out of the fire's path. He, Chop, and Mr. Arborcide inhaled some smoke before making it to the farm's fields. It was a rough ride down, but they were unharmed.

The other searchers were lucky. Not once did the wind stop blowing from the southeast. Mr. Showalter's directions, to head south and then east, saved them all from getting into trouble escaping the blaze. The ladies were the first to make it down to the Horst's field and waited at the edge of the woods worrying. Their worry didn't last long. Deborah and Dunlap knew instinctively that the fire was dangerous and ran sure-footed, delivering their riders safely home. This full-speed ride through the forest was very unnerving for Mr. Alder and Mr. Horst because they were worrying about keeping the children safe. For their part, the children were only thinking about holding on for dear life. If these riders had known how confident the horses felt as they performed their duty, then all of them would have rested easier. When the horses finally got to the   bottom of the Horst's wooded hill, the riders let out huge sighs of relief as they dismounted. Mrs. Alder and Mrs. Horst ran to hug their families.

Once reunited, the searchers stood around—still dazed from the wonder of the bright light. Mr. Horst said something about getting more distance between them and the fire hazard—about going to the farmhouse. Mr. Alder radioed Ranger Bob and found out he was safely at the Arborcide farm. He informed Bob that everyone had made it out safely, except for the dogs. They were still missing. Bob told Mr. Alder that he'd come over as soon as they got the fire under control. A team of fire-fighting rangers would be going in on the ground once the tanker planes had things under control.

Miss Anne, Matty, and Ryker were standing apart from the others and staring in the direction of the blaze. Their friends were still in the woods, perhaps unable to escape the inferno. As they thought about this, each of them started to cry.

Mrs. Alder went up to Matty and Ryker and stroked their hair. She said, "My dear ones. You don't know how happy I was to see you come out of the forest safely with your father. We'll have to pray that Amos can do the same."

"And Beauregard too, Mom," said Matty.

"And Beauregard too," she added.

Miss Sue approached Miss Anne, who was still crying, and said. "I'm sorry, my friend. I shouldn't have risked Beau's life just because of my anger toward that old man. I'm so sorry."

Miss Anne wasn't mad at her friend. She just wanted her boy to come back. She hugged Miss Sue and cried some more. As Sue looked over her shoulder toward the fire, she saw two sparkling lights at the top of the hill. She said, "What in the world is that?"

As everyone looked up, they saw lights—like handfuls of bluish-yellow sparklers—starting to descend from the top of the hill. They looked closer and recognized what was carrying the lights. It was the lost friends. Beauregard had found Amos, and they were coming home—alive!

"It's Amos and Beauregard!" Ryker shouted. "But what are they carrying?"

Matty dashed to meet them and everyone followed. The dogs were moving slowly because of their wounds. Mr. Alder caught up with Matty, lifted her in his arms, and ran up the hill to the dogs. The dogs collapsed when Matty and Mr. Alder reached them.

"They're bleeding, Dad," Matty said. Mr. Alder set his daughter down, turned to Mr. Horst, who was still down the hill, and said, "Nelson, we're going to need a wagon for these two. They're hurt badly. And you better call a vet."

"I'll get the tractor and be back," he shouted. He jumped onto Dunlap, grabbed Deborah's reins, and went to the barn with the horses.

Mr. Alder and Matty stared at the sparking sticks. Ryker came up behind them and peeked around. "Look at all that blood. Are they going to be okay, Dad?" he asked.

"I don't know, Son. Let's concentrate on getting them back to the house right now."

"What are those sticks they've got?" Ryker asked.

"I'm not sure," said Mr. Alder.

Matty recognized what they were holding, even though she had never expected to see it in two pieces. She said to her father, "It's the magic wand, but it's broken!" She gently stroked the fuzzy spot behind Amos' ear and lifted the stick from his mouth, then did the same with Beauregard. She held the sparking ends away from her and cautiously touched the sparks. Matty found that the sparks were bright but not hot. Whatever doubts Mr. Alder had had about the magic wand dissolved as he saw the sparking sticks. They confirmed the children's story for him. He started to tend to the dog's wounds, but his eyes kept moving back to the sticks.

The ladies arrived. Miss Anne got on her knees and hugged Beauregard. He licked her forearms as she petted his head. Mrs. Alder helped Mr. Alder slow some of the bleeding by tearing her bandanna into strips to use for bandages. When she saw the sparking sticks, she knew that this was the wand Matty and Ryker had talked about. She didn't know what was happening to it, but there was no mistaking what it was.

Miss Sue asked, "What did you take from the dogs, Matty?"

Matty said, "It's the Samurai sword stick we showed you the other day. It's broken, though."

Miss Anne perked up her ears and asked, "Your Samurai sword stick? And broken?"

"Yes, Miss Anne. It's been broken somehow. And it's giving off all these sparks." Matty had forgotten all about holding the stick with her bare hand. There was too much going on now. She was really worried about her friend. He wasn't looking very good. She stuffed the sparking sticks into her backpack and concentrated on helping her dad with Amos.

Mr. Horst returned with the tractor and hay wagon. He rushed up the hill and helped Mr. Alder carry the dogs down one at a time. They loaded them onto the back of the wagon, resting them on soft piles of fresh hay.

"I was able to catch Dr. Dingledine on his cell phone," Mr. Horst said smiling. "He just gave me the number last week. I don't know about these gadgets, but he said he's on the road and heading right over. Can't complain about that."

As they were riding back to the barn, Mr. Alder called Ranger Bob again. "Bob, how are you doing with the fire?"

"John's been directing things from the air. Walsh's people have it just about out. I'm going in with a cleanup crew in a minute. The sheriff's deputy is here at Arbor-cides' now. She'll hold onto these two until we figure out what to do with them.

"I've got good news. The dogs came out of the forest. They're pretty chewed up, but they're alive," Mr. Alder told him.

"That's great, Ben. I've got to get going. I'll come over and meet up with you as soon as I can."

"Okay, Bob, we'll wait at the Horst's until you get back over. Call if you get held up."

"Right. I'll be in touch."

The tractor stopped in front of the house and every-one got off—except the dogs. Mr. Alder figured the wagon would be as good a place as any for the vet to check them over. They didn't have to wait long for him either. He drove into the lane soon after they'd stopped. Dr. Dingledine did some triage on the dogs and said he thought they would both recover fully. The bites and lacerations would need stitches, so he wanted to get them back to the animal hospital. "I don't work on small animals much," the vet said. "That's my partner's specialty. I want to get them over to our clinic and get him working on them." He gave the dogs some pain medicine, then the men loaded Amos and Beauregard into his van. Dr. Dingledine said it would be best if everyone waited a few hours before coming to visit the animals. Amos and Beauregard would need to be sedated in order to get them all stitched up. "Why don't you stop by this evening? They'll be in a good place then. We'll need to keep them overnight, I think." After saying this, he loaded up the dogs and sped off to the clinic.

Miss Sue said, "I think at least *one* of us ought to be there." So after appointing herself to keep watch on Amos and Beauregard, she drove off to the clinic.

When she had gone, Mrs. Horst invited everyone inside to rest and eat something while they waited on Ranger Bob. It was now afternoon and they could all see the smoke rising into the air in the distance. Mr. Showalter was high above directing the operation as the fire-fighting planes dropped loads of water and fire retardant.

It was a long time before Ranger Bob came to the Horst's farm. After eating and talking, the Horsts went out to tend to some farm chores, and Miss Anne took a little snooze in the parlor of the farmhouse. The Alders left Anne resting and took a walk around the barn area. Matty remembered the broken sticks. She brought them out for her family to look at. They had stopped sparking completely now. Ryker said, "Do you think they still work?"

"I don't know," Matty said. She took one stick in her hand and looking at her parents, struck the ground with it. Nothing happened. She tried both sticks together. Again, nothing. The magic seemed to be gone from them.

"They don't work anymore," she said, almost in tears.

"Maybe they can be fixed," her dad told her in an attempt to cheer her up. Just then Ranger Bob pulled in the driveway. Matty put the sticks away dejectedly. The broken stick was one last disappointment in what had been a truly awful day.

The Alders walked back toward the house to meet Ranger Bob. The afternoon was getting on now. Miss Anne had heard the truck coming down the driveway and came out of the house. The Horsts were coming up from the barn to meet them all. When they saw Bob get out of his truck, they thought he looked as if he'd seen a ghost. He had grime and soot all over him and was still wearing his fire-fighting gear. There had been a lot of work to do on the ground after the planes had put out most of the fire. Bob stood in the driveway with them and gave the following account. What they heard gave everyone chills.

"We got to the area where the fire had started and everything was burnt to a crisp. It's been so dry because of the drought this winter, and the fire had quite a bit of help from Buzz. Seems the Arborcides have been running a secret mill back in there. When they thought we were going to discover it, Buzz spread gasoline all around, and torched the place. We found their flatbed truck loaded with milling equipment nearby. It's a heap of warped metal now. Got bowed every which way by the heat.

"Old man Arborcide has confessed to all of this. He's pretty devastated right now. That brings me to the worst of it. Buzz Arborcide is dead. Got caught in the fire . . . him and his dog. That vicious dog we thought was wild? Well it was Buzz's watchdog at the mill. Old man Arborcide says he sicced him on us today to scare us off.

"I'm not sure what to make of how we found them. Buzz and his dog were all hung up in some kind of thorny mass of twisted trees. They're like nothing I've ever seen. You couldn't have built a stronger cage if you'd tried. The fire didn't even touch the wood, just left it a little scorched. The stuff's like steel."

The ranger paused and looked at the ground shaking his head. "I don't know what to say. A man died today because he was greedy. Now his Pa and brother are going to jail . . . " He paused again, then continued, "The mill is ashes, except for the corrugated roof and a couple of bicycles lying next to it."

"Did you say *bicycles*, Ranger Bob?" Matty asked.

"Yes. The boys had a couple of small bicycles up there. Is that important?"

"We forgot to tell you, Bob," Mr. Alder said. "So much was happening earlier in the week. The kids had their bikes stolen at your station on Sunday afternoon. They said a big truck stopped and then sped off, but they didn't get a look at it."

"I'll ask Chop about it. Knowing them, they probably *did* take the bikes. Chop admitted to being in the forest on Tuesday with Buzz. They were the ones who hit Amos and took off. We interrupted their tree stealing. They tried to hide, but Amos sniffed them out."

Ranger Bob paused and removed his hat, then continued, "Now the strangest part of Chop's story is this: He told me about a magic stick that could grow trees. Says that's what they sent the dog to take from Matty. When Amos chased after him, the boys caught Amos and locked him up at the mill. Chop doesn't have any idea how his brother could have gotten caught in those thorns. Didn't believe me when I told him about them. Had to see them for himself."

The Alders looked at each other and knew what they had to do. No more secrets! Matty pulled the broken pieces of the magic wand from her backpack. She handed them to Ranger Bob, and slowly the entire family told Bob all the things that had happened to them during the week. He stopped them often with questions and they answered all of them. When they finished, Bob slapped his hat against his leg a few times, and then scratched his head a long while.

"That's the wildest story I've ever heard tell of. Normally I'd say you all were off your rockers, but I've seen some bizarre things today. That light for one. And that thorny cage Buzz got trapped in. Been puzzling over them since I saw 'em. Makes your story not sound so unbelievable."

Miss Anne was taking all this in. She'd had an idea that the stick was special since she'd seen it on Saturday evening. But she thought it was merely a memento—a sign—not something possessing the kind of powers the Alders were describing. She remembered the words of the old rhyme:

From the stump a stem shall grow,
　　Bent like a soul in pain.
It is a sign of hope reborn,
　　A forest where life seems vain.

Hold the wand with care ye saints,
　　For it contains the future,
Of grove and stand and wood alike,
　　In this we must but be sure.

But what does it mean? she wondered. It was a question she would find herself asking often in the days ahead as she talked about the stick with Miss Sue and the Alders.

The Horsts, meanwhile, didn't know whether to believe the story or attribute it to the work of the devil. The Alders kept using the word "magical," and that bothered them. "Magic" was something good people weren't supposed to be messing around with. The Horsts didn't say anything. They were very reserved people when it came to expressing their opinion about such things. But later that night, they did pray for the Alder children and their parents.

Ranger Bob didn't have time to stand around contemplating the significance of what had happened. He needed to go and check on the cleanup team and then head over to talk with the sheriff and county attorney. He said his good-byes and arranged to come to the Alders' home the next morning to talk.

After Ranger Bob had left, the Alders and Miss Anne said good-bye to the Horsts, thanking them for all their help. They jumped into the car together. Miss Anne was going to ride over with them to check on the animals and meet Miss Sue. The Horsts were glad that the Alders had found Amos. This seemed to be the only bright spot in a day where it had been revealed that their neighbors were thieves and one of them was now dead. Mr. and Mrs. Horst wouldn't have time to think about this or the magic tree wand, though, because soon they would be caught up in their evening work of milking the dairy herd.

Amos and Beauregard were asleep in separate kennels when the gang arrived to see them. They found Miss Sue in the kennel room, sitting on a chair reading some pet magazines. The nurse who led them back to Miss Sue allowed Matty and Ryker to open Amos' kennel and crawl in to pet him. He didn't rouse as they kissed his head and stroked his tummy.

"I love this little guy," Ryker said to his sister.

"I love him too, Ryker. I'm so glad he's going to be okay. You know he's my best friend—along with you."

"Mine too, along with you."

Miss Anne didn't crawl into Beauregard's kennel—for one thing she was too big. She was content to reach in and stroke his head and long ears. She was proud of him for finding Amos today. She didn't know what he had done, but imagined it was probably something heroic. No one besides Amos would ever know about it, but Beauregard *had* done something truly heroic.

After checking in with the vet and being told that both the dogs could go home tomorrow, the Alders and the ladies went home. Everyone was ready to relax. The ladies spent a quiet evening. Each took a hot bubble bath and then they sat together in the dark listening to a CD of Vivaldi. The Alders were so tired they splurged and called out for pizza from Luigi's. Mr. Alder and Ryker drove into town to pick it up while the gals took showers. That evening the children talked with their parents about the events of the week. The family took turns feeling the broken pieces of the magic wand, wondering where it had come from. Each time they touched the stick, Matty and Ryker couldn't help feeling guilty about what they'd done and the harm it had caused. They even wondered if Buzz Arborcide's death was their fault. Mr. and Mrs. Alder talked a long time with their children about these things, but couldn't offer the children any solid answers to their questions. Late in the evening, they decided that answers would have to wait until tomorrow. Their bodies needed rest now even more than their minds needed answers.

Matty put the pieces of the magic tree wand in her backpack and stored it under her bed. When she lay down, she started to cry as images of the day came into her mind. She was especially frightened when she thought about the man and dog that had died. Ryker came to her doorway not long after she'd lain down. He had his comforter and pillow in his hands.

"Matty, are you crying?"

"Yes, Ryker, but I'm okay."

"Do you mind if I sleep in here tonight?"

"No. That would be nice."

Ryker stretched his comforter on the floor in Amos' spot and wrapped up in it. Matty talked with her brother about how nice it would be to have Amos back home. This was the second night he'd not slept beside her bed. And tonight there was no magic tree wand under the bed—only a broken stick that had lost all its spark.

Mr. Alder went early the next morning to pick up Amos before Matty and Ryker woke up. Their friend was still very weak from the battles and beatings of the last two days. He ached all over and rode quietly home, lying on the backseat of the car.

As Mr. Alder pulled into the driveway, Matty and Ryker flew out of the mud room to greet them. Mr. Alder reached over the seat and pushed open Amos' car door. He hobbled out of the car and into the children's open arms. Matty and Ryker knelt nuzzling his head and gently stroking his fur. They told him how brave he'd been and how glad they were to have him home alive, then Mr. Alder suggested they help Amos inside to rest.

The kids stayed with Amos most of the day, giving him scraps of chicken and pieces of cheese. Ranger Bob came by mid-morning and had coffee with the Alders. He listened again to some of the stories from the week and found out that the magic wand couldn't grow trees anymore. He told the Alders that Mr. Arborcide and Chop had signed a confession about the tree thefts in the National Forest. And Bob had some exciting information for the children. He told them, "Matty, Ryker, the county attorney asked me who ought to get the reward for the capture of the thieves. I told him that you two and Amos were the ones who found them out. So, he's going to put your names in for it."

"A reward?" Ryker asked. "What is it?"

"It's two thousand dollars. You will each get half of it. Of course, your mom and dad will be deciding what you use it for."

"That will be a nice addition to your college funds," said Mrs. Alder.

"Oh, Mom," Ryker said dejectedly.

There was a pause in the conversation. Mrs. Alder got some more coffee for Ranger Bob. Then Matty asked, "Ranger Bob, did you get Mr. Arborcide's son out of the thorn bushes?"

"Yes Matty, we did, and also his dog. They called him 'Grinder.' We took Buzz Arborcide over to the funeral home, and buried Grinder at the pet cemetery. Don't you keep fretting over them. You didn't make that happen. They brought it on themselves."

"I know, Ranger Bob. I keep telling myself that, but I feel awful."

"Yes, it's a hard thing."

Mr. Alder changed the conversation and talked about what was going on at church next week. The day after tomorrow was Palm Sunday and Easter was just a week away. Bob told them that he didn't have to work either day and would be able to sit with them at church. Matty and Ryker said they were going to count on it. Finally Ranger Bob said he had to get back to the forest. The rangers were surveying the burned area and a few places the Arborcides had removed trees. They were making plans to ensure that the areas recovered well. He left and the kids returned to their work taking care of Amos, who was glad to be at home in the kitchen on his cushion.

The next week went by slowly for Matty and Ryker. They returned to school Monday morning. At night they weren't allowed to do much besides homework. Their parents had struck a deal with them about making up for all the lying. Matty and Ryker had suggested they do extra work around the house and forego any fun activities for a month. Their parents agreed that this was a fair punishment, and started enforcing the plan on Monday.

It was hard not being able to go anywhere or have any fun adventures. Easter Sunday came around. This was usually a day to celebrate, but the children were miserable when they woke up. Getting Easter candy was something "fun," and everything "fun" had been taken away from them for an entire month. Instead of running downstairs for chocolate, as they usually did on Easter morning, today they shuffled and moped their way down to breakfast.

Amos greeted them at the bottom of the stairs, wagging his tail. He had already devoured his Easter treat— a beef rawhide—and was dancing around as best he could. He wasn't 100 percent well yet, but he was feeling much better than a week ago. Matty and Ryker perked up a bit at the sight of their happy friend, and moved on into the kitchen.

"Look, Ryker!" Matty screamed as she came through the kitchen doorway.

"Chocolate!" he yelled back.

They ran to the counter where their mom and dad had two very large Easter baskets waiting for them, filled with colored eggs, chocolates, and candy. Mr. and Mrs. Alder were sitting in the breakfast nook and smiled at one another.

"Now, you two can't spend all morning eating chocolate. You have to eat your breakfast and then we've got to get to church for Easter services. Ranger Bob is expecting you," Mrs. Alder told them.

"Mom . . . Dad . . . You're the greatest," Matty said as she looked at the basket.

"You know it," Ryker added, his mouth full of chocolate already. Amos was rubbing his nose into their legs hoping for a treat to fall from the baskets.

Later that morning Matty and Ryker went to church with their parents. Ranger Bob met them at the front door and picked them up as they ran into his arms. "Come on, Junior Rangers, they're holding a seat for us inside." How happy they were to be in his arms again! He made them feel almost as safe as their dad did. And sitting with him the service didn't even seem boring today. Of course, Ryker fidgeted and drew pictures on the prayer cards as usual. He even munched on some chocolate that his parents hadn't seen him sneak into his pockets earlier.

After church, Ranger Bob came over for a big turkey lunch with the Alders. It was truly a celebration day for all of them. And their parents told Matty and Ryker that today they were off probation. They could have an adventure later when Ranger Bob left. Bob stayed for a while and played with the kids and Amos in the backyard. When he left, Mr. and Mrs. Alder asked the kids how they wanted to spend the day.

"Can we go play by the lake and in the woods? We haven't been out of the yard all week," Ryker asked.

"Oh, I suppose so. We thought you might want to spend the afternoon with us," Mrs. Alder answered.

"No offense, Mom, but we need to get out. I don't know how I'm going to make it with another three weeks of this probation stuff," Matty said.

"You two go on and get changed into some play clothes. You can go, but we want you back *before* dinnertime," Mr. Alder told them.

The kids changed their clothes and grabbed their backpacks. Matty hadn't touched hers all week. It was too depressing to think about the broken stick that was inside it. They got some water and a few snacks, and quickly stuffed them into their backpacks. Amos knew something was up as he watched this. He was wagging his tail excitedly.

"Mom, do you think Amos is well enough to go with us?" Matty asked.

"Ben, what do you think?"

"I think he'd like to get out. But you can't wrestle him, and you need to take it slowly."

"No wrestling . . . got it, Dad," Ryker said, smiling as he looked playfully at Amos.

They finished packing and headed over to Silver Lake to play. The cattail grasses were greening up and the red winged blackbirds were flitting in and out of them. The friends played near the water, dipping hands and paws in, chasing bugs, and scaring pond trout. When all the secrets of the lake seemed exhausted, Ryker said, "Matty, let's sneak up to Mole Hill for a few minutes. We haven't been up there for a couple of weeks. I bet the whole valley looks green from up there."

"I'm up for it," she said. Matty wanted to get up higher and look around at everything that was growing.

Amos led the way up the hill. There were saplings all along the trail now. Matty started noticing them and said, "Ryker look at all these little trees. We must have planted them when we came down the hill with the stick. We didn't know how it worked then, remember?"

"Yeh, and there are a couple of big ones. You must have been hitting the ground with it."

"I did. I remember I was waving it like a whip antenna."

Amos found the tree he'd run into a couple of weeks before. He sniffed it and it still smelled like him. He marked it again and ran to catch up with Matty and Ryker.

They reached the top of the hill and walked through the stand of oaks at the top. Ryker looked into his "volcano vent" to see if he could find another magic wand—but there wasn't another one.

Matty was sitting on the rock formation where Ryker had proclaimed himself the "Sky-running champion." Amos sat down next to her and waited to have his head scratched. Matty was thinking about the past couple of weeks and she wanted to cry again. She finally decided to take the broken wand out of her backpack for the first time since she'd packed it away. It didn't stick out of the top now that it was broken, so she reached inside and felt the smooth wood. It still made her feel comfortable and safe, like she'd felt holding it in Mr. Showalter's plane. But then she thought, *It's not the same stick now. It's not even a stick . . . it's two sticks.* She pulled the two halves out of the pack to look at them. As she brought the broken ends up out of the sack, she saw something that made her heart jump.

Growing from the splintered ends of each piece of the wand was a small seedling, maybe four or five inches long. They were at an angle to the stick. They'd been growing against the bottom of the backpack and had nowhere to go. The roots of the seedling were intermingled with the splintered shreds of the sticks. Matty felt one of them and, as she stroked it, it fell off into her hand.

As she watched, something magical happened. Another seedling slowly grew out from the splinters. It grew four- or five-inches long and stopped. She switched sticks and tried this again. The same thing happened. Amos sat next to her sniffing her hands, the sticks, and the saplings. He was very intrigued by what he smelled. He wanted to grab the sticks and play tug-o-war with Matty, just like on the day he'd found the whole stick.

"Ryker, come here!" Matty yelled. He came over and she explained what was happening.

"Let me try," he said, and pulled the seedling off the end of the stick. Another one grew out slowly. He started doing this over and over and over. The more he pulled them the faster they grew. He kept this up, as if he were trying to pull all the tissues rapidly out of a box one at a time.

Matty finally shouted, "Ryker! *Stop!*"

"Why? This is cool!"

"Because we're going to have to plant all of those, and we don't have all day."

"What are you talking about?"

"Don't you see, Ryker? The stick is still working. It's growing trees the best it can. And they're still magical trees. We've got to plant them."

Ryker scratched his head and thought a moment. Then he said, "I liked it better the other way. All you had to do was hit the ground. This new way seems like a whole lot of work."

"Ryker, are you *always* such a wimp? The stick's still giving us a way to do everything we'd thought about before. We can replant the forest with it. It's just going to take a little longer . . . that's all."

Ryker thought this over for a few minutes. He pulled a couple more seedlings off and said, "You're right. This will work. But it *is* going to be a lot of work. And we'll see who the wimp is when it comes to planting." He walked over and started digging with his hands in the dirt. One-by-one he planted the seedlings he had. Amos came over and even helped him dig some holes. Matty smiled at her brother. He was a pain in the neck sometimes, but if she waited long enough, he usually got things—usually even better than *she* did. She walked over and planted her seedlings as well.

Ryker finished and stood up. He said, "Matty? We've got to tell Ranger Bob and Mom and Dad. No secrets. Remember?"

"I remember. And I *want* to tell them."

"Good. We can start our work by replanting the area that was burned," he said with excitement.

Matty was getting excited herself and said, "And then we can replant the places where the Arborcides stole trees."

"The possibilities are endless, Sis . . . that is, if we work hard."

"I can work hard. What about you Amos?"

Amos looked up. He was still sniffing around at all the young saplings and freshly dug dirt. He stared at his friends and then marked a little sycamore sapling. Matty and Ryker laughed so loudly at this that Amos stopped his marking.

"Matty! He can be the guy to fertilize the seedlings after we plant 'em," Ryker said. Ryker got so tickled laughing about this that tears came to his eyes.

Matty giggled uncontrollably along with her brother. Amos, not wanting to miss out on the fun, came up and started walking between their legs and nuzzling them. Ryker grabbed Amos' front paws and lifted him to his feet. The three friends started dancing in a circle singing their Famous Amos song:

Doot! Doot! Doot!
    Famous Amos, he's the dog for us.
Doot! Doot! Doot!
    Famous Amos, our dog don't make no fuss.
Doot! Doot! Doot!
    Famous Amos, he's the dog for me (and me!)

He's famous, Famous Amos, we love him yesiree.
Love him yes-sir-ree.

After a few choruses of Amos' theme song, the three friends rushed down the hill toward town. They wanted to tell everyone that the magic tree wand still had some magic left.

Visit the Website

www.magictreewand.com

Famous Amos

Madelen, Ryker & Marty Bullis

Piano

Fa mous A mos,   Fa mous A

he's the   dog for us.

mos,   Fa mous A mos,

our dog don't make no fuss.   he's

He's fa mous, Fa mous A mos,   We

the dog for me.   love him

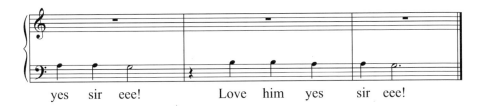

yes sir eee!   Love him yes sir eee!

Famous Amos

Alternate

Madelen, Ryker & Marty Bullis

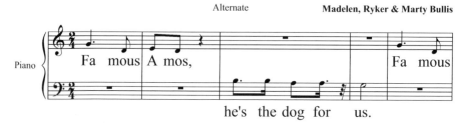

Piano

Fa mous A mos,   Fa mous

he's the dog for us.

A mos,   Fa mous A mos,

our dog don't make no fuss.

me. He's fa mous, Fa mous A mos, we

he's the dog for

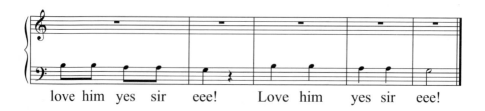

love him yes sir eee! Love him yes sir eee!

2677936